..., six for gold,
Seven for a secret never to be told . . .

for a 3 Girl

Jenny Oldfield

*Hodder
Children's
Books*

a division of Hodder Headline plc

1

Bounce-bounce-step-bounce. Shoot! Whack. The ball hits the board and shimmies through the hoop into the basket.

High-five! Carter smacks Ziggy's palm and gives a skip and a jump. Sporting superstars – not!

Carter's trying out for the basketball team in his regulation faded baggy shorts and sweatshirt, Zig's wearing a new pair of trainers that glow in the dark.

We girls, meanwhile, are on the adjoining tennis courts practising our forehand drives.

'Follow through, Kate Brennan!' Miss Slay our Sport teacher snarls. Martha Slay: six feet of tanned, rippling sinews and muscle.

I *am* following through, swinging my racket like crazy. But the bright yellow, furry missile hits the net and thuds to the ground. Funny; I used to be good at this game until Miss Slay sank her fangs into me.

'Get into position, Kate. Use your feet. Keep your eye on the ball!'

I am. *I am.*

Bounce-bounce-whoosh! Zig puts another one in the net. At six one and a hundred and fifty pounds, there's nothing complicated. His legs go on forever, he just has to keep a hold of the ball and spring up to lob it into the net. He's in the team for sure.

Unlike Carter, who's a couple of inches shorter and lacks Zig's confidence. I watch him congratulate the scorer again, looking like he wished he was somewhere else.

'Kate Brennan, keep your mind on what you're doing, please!' Miss Slay again. She's a killer, a slave-driver, a tyrant. She thinks we all want to play tennis like Lola Kodak.

You know Lola Kodak. The Golden Girl of American tennis. The nineteen-year-old rising star of the Grand Slam circuit, world ranking number five in the women's game; she of the thick, flame-red ponytail and risqué, figure-hugging sports outfits.

She has a forehand drive that would knock you into next week. And she used to attend school here at Fortune City High.

'Question!' Carter asked for our attention.

We'd showered after tennis and basketball practice and were all hanging round the school gate waiting for the bus; me, Zoey, Connie, Zig and Carter.

'No, stop him please, someone. My brain hurts!' Zoey sighed. She could tell Joey was about to steer us off course into one of his minor insanities.

'Hey!' he said, giving Zoey a crushing look. 'Listen. The question is this: do we issue Ziggy with a passport along with his team shirt?'

'Huh?' Connie was hooked right away. She hated sport and everything associated, but she liked Joey Carter. She was prepared to humour him now. 'How come?'

Carter nursed a secret smile. 'You need a passport to leave the country, right?'

'Yeah . . . ?' Connie still didn't get it.

'So, Zig jumps so high when he puts the ball in the net that it has to be officially considered as leaving American territory. Hence he needs an exit visa, he's subject to immigration control and all that stuff!' Carter tried to look serious for Connie's benefit.

'No-oh!' She knew this couldn't make sense, but in a way it was true; Ziggy definitely launched himself clear of *terra firma*.

The rest of us were grinning as the yellow bus approached.

'Yeah!' Carter insisted. 'When you jump into the air as high as Zig, you leave the country. It's logical; it's like flying in an aeroplane!'

3

'No way.' When Connie shakes her head, her silver earrings glitter and jangle.

I rescued her before the bus drew up. 'But he's still in American airspace,' I pointed out. 'So no passport necessary!'

Carter and I climbed on the bus to head up State Hill towards Constitution Square, leaving Zig the Basketball Pilot, Connie the Confused and Zoey the Unimpressed standing on the sidewalk. They headed downtown towards East Village, where they live.

The bus was crowded, so Carter and I had no choice but to stand in the aisle beside Miss Slay and another teacher, Miss McKee.

'. . . I gave her three golden rules.' Martha Slay was bragging about Lola Kodak as usual. Like Lola was her protégé, like she alone was responsible for her being number five in the women's game.

Whereas everyone knew that Lola's parents had paid for private tennis coaching since she was a little kid, that her uncle, Tomas Lendlova, had been her full-time coach for six years and that the girl was only nineteen now. It had been tennis for breakfast, lunch and dinner ever since the poor kid could remember, and Miss Slay's input had been the occasional hors d'oeuvre, if you get my point. Still, I shouldn't really take it away. Except that she does go on about it.

'. . . Three golden rules,' she insisted. 'I said to her, "Watch the ball. Hit it on the rise. Go for the winning shot." '

' "Watch . . . Hit . . . Go for!" ' Carter mouthed the beginning of each sentence. He'd heard it all a million times before, like the rest of us.

The bus shuddered to a halt beside Fortune Park and let people off.

'I said, "There are three qualities necessary for you to make it to the top: power, consistency, resourcefulness." ' Miss Slay chanted her mantra.

Mousy Miss McKee, the Biology expert, grabbed her chance and made a quick exit at the park stop.

So Slay pounced on me and Carter, giving us an extra repeat-episode of the Lola Kodak legend. 'You never saw anyone work on her topspin the way Lola did! Hour after hour on the school court, weekends, evenings, even during her vacation. That's dedication for you. And her serve was explosive. Over a hundred miles per hour by the age of fifteen. Phenomenal.'

Lola-Lola-Lola! Carter raised his eyebrows at me.

The reason Miss Slay was so obsessed was that in two days' time Lola was to grace us with a visit. The school, I mean. Three years after she left to become a full-time tennis professional, Lola Kodak was finding time in her busy schedule to come back and present the prizes in an inter-school basketball tournament.

We were all going to get a glimpse of Fortune City High's most famous product.

The Sport teacher was to sit beside her during the presentation.

The national Press would be there. Oh, and my dad's TV crew, along with Angel Christian herself.

I should've mentioned that sooner. It was a major reason why Martha Slay was on a high.

Angel had moved on from chat shows and was making a documentary series on sporting heroes. My dad's her producer. Lights, camera, action!

Angelworks has a production unit at the star's palatial home, Heaven's Gate. The house overlooks Fortune Park, and is where me and my dad were headed later that evening.

'You could stay home, hang out with the guys, eat pizza,' Dad had suggested. Eating pizza is code for taking time out, being sociable, doing a little harmless flirting. My father is a shade over-protective in that way.

It's usually Ziggy's name he mentions on the flirting front; like he wants us two to become an item. I tell him that Zig and Zoey already got it together. Zoey wears a silver snake-bracelet engraved with Zig's name.

Dad turns a deaf ear. He likes Zig because Ziggy can be polite; yes sir, no sir, and he agrees with whatever you say. Ideal boyfriend material.

My dad doesn't mention Carter in this pizza-eating context. Joey's manners aren't so good. And he never pushes himself forward.

You can overlook him completely, until you notice his weird sense of humour and his dark blue eyes which study you pretty hard. I notice those things about Joey. Joey knows I notice. But neither of us mentions the fact. That's the way we are together; Kate and Carter – something going on, but no one admitting it.

Anyhow, that night I said I'd skip the pizza and come with Dad. I was sufficiently interested in the Lola Kodak thing to come along and watch him edit tape.

'Sean, Kate, come on in!' Angel greeted us with relief, surrounded by unedited material which she was feeding into machines and watching onscreen. Monitors were banked around the room, showing pictures of Lola Kodak in action on court, Lola Kodak being interviewed by Angel, Lola Kodak winning the French Junior Championship four years earlier, Lola Kodak driving her sponsored Mercedes Benz. 'We already have way too much for next Tuesday's programme,' she told my dad. 'And we still have to film her at this local school presentation on Saturday.'

Dad did his calming, laid-back thing. 'So we cut back on the tennis action,' he suggested, sitting at the control panel. 'This documentary should focus on the personality behind the high-achieving sports person; a more private angle. That's why we want to use more of you and Lola together.'

Dad can flatter Angel's giant ego. He's been her producer for ten years, and you don't survive that experience without knowing how to handle the superstar temperament.

Didn't I tell you about Angel yet? OK; she's small, super-slim, with great big brown eyes and glossy dark hair. She's designed for TV. She lights up when the camera is on her, pulls you in, makes you feel like you're her best buddy. And she regularly makes fifteen million viewers on her new documentary series. That's megabucks for Angelworks, which is her own company. Which is how come she can afford Heaven's Gate and a staff to run the place: housekeeper, personal assistant, driver . . . you name it.

Anyhow, we gathered round Dad and concentrated on the one tape. It showed Angel sitting with Lola on an airplane, en route to Wimbledon. The two were talking as if they'd known each other all their lives.

'So, Lola, tell us a little about your life before the tennis really took off. Lola Kodak, pre-fame and fortune!' (Angel smiling and wheedling.)

'I was a pretty normal kid, I guess.' (Lola shrugging. Lola tongue-tied, not able to put her life into a catchy soundbite.)

(Angel prompting, still smiling.) 'So where did the unusual name come from?'

'My dad's Czechoslovakian. He came over in the sixties and settled in Fortune City. He's a qualified paediatric surgeon and my mom was a nurse in the hospital where he worked. She'd come over from Czechoslovakia a couple of years earlier. Her whole family came because her brother, my uncle, Tomas Lendlova, was already playing the professional tennis circuit. He'd settled in the US and wanted to bring his parents and sister across.' (Lola dealing with straight facts, no problem.)

'She doesn't give it out much,' Angel muttered as Dad played the tape.

I saw what she meant. Unlike Angel, Lola had no love affair with the camera. Her face was pretty but closed; pale complexion like most redheads, freckled by the sun, wide mouth, light grey eyes. And that red hair which she wore loose when she wasn't on court. A lot of women tennis players do that; their long hair

9

letting you know they can be feminine and attractive, that it's not all sweat and pumping iron.

'We'll pick up on that suspicion, that reserve,' Dad suggested. 'She's known for not showing her emotions on court, and if we can portray it off-duty as well, it makes for an interesting subject.'

Angel listened and nodded. 'Like, the enigma of Lola Kodak. What makes her tick? We can do a little probing, hope that she gives us something that she hasn't shown in public before.'

To me this sounded painful, like surgery without an anaesthetic.

The tape played on, telling us more about Lola's famous tennis-playing uncle; how he'd failed to fulfil his early promise as a junior champion, faded from the limelight then reappeared in the early nineties as Lola's full-time coach.

We saw snatches of Tomas Lendlova playing with an old-fashioned wooden racket, his dark hair long and floppy, his heavy eyebrows knotted in concentration, a scowl on his high-cheekboned face. Then we saw him short-haired and up-to-date, twenty-five years older, coaching a skinny kid wearing braces and pigtails; a piece of home-video which the Kodaks had handed over to the film crew for inclusion in the documentary.

'You'd get good pretty fast if Tomas Lendlova was

coaching you,' Angel murmured. '*I'd* get good, and I never held a racket in my life!'

From which I guessed she meant Uncle Tomas was a bit of a slave-driver. Like Miss Slay, only worse because you had him on your back permanently. I don't know the guy personally, but I could see what she was getting at.

Tomas Lendlova was lean and intense. He looked like he had a mouth full of canine teeth. The word 'Wolf' came to mind when you watched him prowl around the tennis court.

'OK, so we look at the relationship between uncle and niece,' Dad concluded. 'Once we've covered the rapid rise, the championships, the ranking, we go back to the crucial influence of Tomas Lendlova.'

'Good.' Angel nodded. 'And we end with a big question mark over the amount of pressure he puts her under.'

Dad made a note, stopping the tape on a frame which showed Lendlova standing behind Lola just after she'd won the French Junior Championship for the first time. They were facing camera, close-up. She was holding up a silver trophy, smiling and exhausted.

The smile didn't quite hide the fact that Lola was crying. Not tears of joy, I should say. More like relief and defiance mixed. 'OK, so I did it. I did what you

11

pushed and pummelled and shaped me into achieving. Now, for God's sake, let me be!'

And Uncle Tomas hovered at her shoulder, long, lined face, hair cropped close to the scalp, no smile. He was looking sideways, his eyes boring into the back of Lola's head. '*You think you're through. You imagine you're champion and I'm done with you . . . No way, Lola honey. This is only the beginning. Believe me!*'

It made me shudder and be grateful that I was never going to be the Golden Girl. Miss Slay could yell at me all she liked to punch that volley straight at my opponent. I just didn't have the killer instinct. And no Uncle Tomas.

' "Watch this face!" ' Angel whispered, leaning close to the screen. 'Let's make that our closing shot; girl under pressure and likely to crack!'

2

Let me start by saying that I live with my mom and dad, my older sister, Marcie, and my kid brother, Damien, at number 342 Twenty-second Street.

The thing is, we're in Marytown, the old Italian quarter of Fortune City. It's run-down. The most excitement you get on Twenty-second Street is when the neighbour's cat falls fifteen floors and lands on its feet on the roof of Mr Alsip's Toyota. 'Lucky Black Cat Escapes Unharmed.' Or when the deli on the corner wins a prize for the best pastrami on rye. 'Local Sandwich-Maker Scoops Trophy.' You know the kind of garbage.

So, Thursday afternoon turned out, without my knowing it, to be one big, I mean BIG day.

I got off the school bus with Kate, walked with her across Constitution Square, said goodbye and came on home. 'Hey, Joey,' Damien said to me, coming down the stoop two steps at a time. He had a mouth full of cookies and a can of ice-cold Coke in one hand.

'Hey, Dame.' I swung in through the door, dumped my bag and headed for my room.

I wasn't expecting anything out of the ordinary.

There was music coming from the basement; my sister sings in a band and they rehearse down there. The TV in the living-room was playing to no one in particular, an audience was laughing at jokes that definitely weren't funny.

'Joey, pick up your bag!' Mom called after me up the stairs.

'Yeah, yeah.' Later.

'Someone's gonna break a leg! What do you have in here; a dead body?' Mom was lifting the heavy bag, giving me a hard time, when the bathroom door opened.

And out walked Lola Kodak.

Yeah, I know. But wait.

Lola Kodak, as in world-famous tennis player. Also, Lola Kodak, as in one-time best friend of my sister, Marcie.

They went to school together. Their paths parted pretty dramatically at the age of sixteen, when Marcie joined the band and Lola went off to play the circuit. But before that, they had a lot in common.

The way I remember it, they liked the same clothes, the same boys, the same music. Lola was always round at our house before she was famous, or Marcie was round at hers. Not that I think Lola's parents, Dr and Mrs Kodak, favoured the arrangement. Marcie wasn't sporty enough for their taste, and my family doesn't have much money.

Uncool address. Blue-collar workers. But the girls didn't let that get in the way.

They swapped dresses, tried on make-up and did things with their hair. Don't ask me; I was too young to notice.

That was three years ago. Since then, nothing.

Lola went to Paris and won the Junior Championship. I remember Marcie was pleased and sad. She said Lola would never come back to Fortune City High, and she was right.

'Write her nice, chatty letters,' Mom advised at first. 'She needs to hear from her old friends at school.'

Marcie wrote with the gossip and got no replies.

'I'm sure she appreciates them anyway,' Mom told my big sister, who once cried because Lola had dropped her big-time. 'But imagine how busy she must be, how much pressure she must be under . . . Is it any wonder she doesn't write back?'

So what was Lola Kodak doing standing in my bathroom door? I guess I let my jaw drop and a stupefied expression must have crept on to my face, because the Golden Girl cracked a grin and said, 'Hey, Joey. Remember me?'

It turned out she was sick of hotels. She was coming home for the schools basketball final, but her parents had recently moved house to Lancaster, Pennsylvania. So she'd decided to look Marcie up to see if she could stay at our place.

'Nobody tells me anything!' I muttered. (Master of the obvious; that's me.)

'Nobody told me either, until Lola showed up on the doorstep,' Mom hissed back, dragging me downstairs to explain that she'd given Lola my room, and my bed for the next two days was the living-room sofa. 'I don't think even Marcie knew until midday today!'

'Yeah, and by tonight, the whole world will be in on it. We won't be able to get out of the house for Press!' Lola Kodak was such hot news right now that they'd be camping on the stoop, out on the sidewalk, taking pictures with zoom lenses from the apartment block across the street.

Marcie heard me going on about it as she came into the kitchen for a tub of ice-cream and two teaspoons. Girltalk in her bedroom was obviously scheduled in before supper. 'No one knows where Lola's staying,' she said, nose in the air. 'This is time-out for her, so she gets the chance to be a normal person again.'

Like, yeah. Like, what happened to the three years when Lola snubbed the Carters?

None of that mattered to Marcie now. She and the ice-cream were halfway up the stairs, my mom was smiling and, bemused, I was already checking the sidewalk for signs of the first journalist.

We made it until Friday morning, then Damien blew it.

The stupid kid boasted to his friend, Ben, who sits next to him in class, that we had a world-famous sports star staying at our place.

'Yeah, like Michael Jordan!' Ben sneered.

Well, you wouldn't believe it either, if you're honest.

'Guess again,' Damien said. 'Clue number one; not basketball.'

'Baseball?'

'Nope.'

'What then?'

'Tennis. Woman. Venus Williams . . . not!' Damien must have thought he was being smart.

'Lola Kodak!' Ben got it in one, jumped up from his seat and told the world. He yelled it out. 'Lola Kodak is staying at Damien Carter's house!'

Miss Slay, who happens to be Damien's class teacher, was on to it in a flash. She extracted information like a dentist takes out teeth: street, house number, since when and for how long?

By mid-morning break it was all round the school.

By lunchtime the posse of pressmen was pounding on our door.

I got home at four and had to fight my way through.

'Where exactly is Miss Kodak sleeping?' 'Does she have

a special fitness diet? A workout routine?' 'Is she able to switch off and relax, or has the pressure of the tennis circuit got to her?' The journalists jostled for position as I put my key in the lock and they pressed me for a quote.

'Yeah, she's cracked up. She's a complete wreck. She does drugs and drinks two bottles of vodka a day.'

This is what I felt like saying, just to give them something to write about. Instead, I gritted my teeth, ready to plead the Fifth Amendment.

'We picked up a rumour that Lola's fitness for Flushing Meadow is in doubt!'

This was the main reason why the press pack was out in force. I heard one voice which I recognised above the rest, asking about the start of the American Open on Monday. The voice belonged to Angel Christian, and it had an effect like the Biblical parting of the waves. Even the serious sports journalists gave way to it, letting Angel through in her bright pink linen suit, with her bright pink glossy smile.

A cameraman followed, loaded with equipment, and a soundman, and a producer – Sean Brennan. Oh yeah, Kate had mentioned that Angelworks was doing a documentary on Lola. That would explain them being there on our doorstep.

'Is it true?' Angel asked me again. 'Is there a problem with Lola's fitness?'

I ducked my head, turned the key and managed to slip inside without comment.

'. . . Don't look at me!' I said to Marcie, who confronted me as I flung my bag on the floor.

Lola was hunched on a chair in the basement, listening to a demo tape, not enjoying the prospect of having to face the baying pack at the door.

'Damien!' Marcie breathed fire and flexed her long fingernails. 'He's dead!'

I didn't say anything. But neither did I rate the kid's chances very highly when he finally showed up from school.

So Lola's bid for forty-eight hours of normal life didn't come off, though Damien's head pretty nearly did.

He just about made it out of Marcie's clutches and to the ball game next day.

Along with what seemed like the whole of Fortune City, population three million, who tried to squeeze into the school's sports arena; official capacity two and a half thousand.

' "Ziggy-Ziggy-Ziggy! Zig-Zig-Zig!" '

Zoey was cheerleader for our team. She razzled and dazzled and strutted her stuff before the game.

Kate sat next to me and smiled as Zig led the way on to the court. There were two kids taller than him on the opposing team, but they looked clumsy and slow. Ziggy would weave in and out; no contest. I noticed that he looked deadly serious. Now, for Zig, that was most definitely worrying.

'He's nervous!' I whispered to Kate.

She had her eye on the Angelworks camera team squatting on scaffolding which had been erected on the side-line, especially for the occasion. 'Nervous is good!' she replied. 'Adrenalin shooting through the system and all!'

We were sitting in special seats, immediately behind Marcie and Lola, who were sandwiched between the school principal, Mr Fiorello, to the left, and our very own Miss Slay to the right. There was an important looking guy in a black-and-white Adidas top on the Sport teacher's right hand side who I didn't recognise. When I asked Kate about him, she said it was Lola's coach, Tomas Lendlova.

'When did he show up?' I was curious; one unsmiling face in a happy crowd kind of draws the attention.

Never mind that the whistle had gone, the game had started, and Ziggy was loping down the middle with the ball.

'Dunno.' Kate gave the coach a glance and pursed her full mouth like she was tasting something sour.

Unsmiling, sitting up straight, probably bored by the

small-time occasion he'd been dragged into. That's the impression I got of Tomas Lendlova. There was a kind of watchdog look about him; a snappiness about the lean jaws. When I whispered this to Kate, she said 'Wolf!' Just like that.

Then Ziggy popped the ball in the basket and we cheered and forgot all about Lendlova until maybe a couple of hours later.

We won the game, 57–43, no problem, thanks to Ziggy.

What a star.

He came and took the trophy from Lola, his face bright red, a grin spreading from ear to ear.

A thousand flashlights blinked and whirred as the tennis star, the local girl made good, shook his hand. The team raised their hands and gave the crowd a two-fisted salute.

I felt terrific for him. The whole of Fortune City High paid homage.

'Will we ever get his feet back on the ground?' Kate murmured across the applause.

The fact that her long dark hair swept sideways across her face and over my bare arm distracted me from Zig and the winning team for a moment. She has this effect. I considered making the passport joke again, but thought better of it. Not that jabbering something about Zig needing a bigger size baseball cap was any better.

When I want to be witty and attractive, I end up rolling my tongue around my mouth and, ape-like, I find difficulty shaping even the simplest sounds. That's life, I guess. You want to come across like Brad Pitt and you end up squeaking like a Munchkin.

By this time, Ziggy and the team were doing a lap of honour, and Miss Slay was bending Lola's ear, big time.

Lola smiled and nodded politely. She glanced at Tomas, her coach, who was already looking at his watch.

'Excuse me a moment,' Lola said to Slay, sidling out along the row. 'I have to use the rest-room.'

'You know where it is!' the tennis teacher quipped. 'You were a student in the school for long enough!' Her attempts at witticisms were no better than mine.

Anyway, I wanted to be in the boys' locker room to congratulate the team when they got there, so I found myself slipping out with Lola, nipping out of the stadium and following her down an empty corridor.

Good time to get her autograph, you might think. I'd promised Zoey I'd do this before the end of the evening. But I had a thing about that. I mean, it must suck to be hunted for your signature twenty-four hours a day, seven days a week, and I didn't want to be like everyone else, hustling and hassling. Give her five minutes of alone-time, I thought, keeping my distance.

Only, she didn't reach the girls' rest-room, like she'd said. She kind of hesitated by the locker-rooms instead. From fifty paces behind, I saw her heave a sigh and lean against the nearest metal locker. Her whole body kind of slumped, as if the effort of smiling and shaking hands and signing her name had all been too much. Her head went forward so that her red hair hid her face and though I couldn't hear any noise, I was pretty sure she'd burst into tears.

Then there were footsteps down another corridor, seemingly heading her off. Something made me step into a classroom doorway, out of sight, from which position my own view was restricted.

But I saw enough to make out the black-and-white sports top worn by Lola's coach. I saw him take his rising star roughly by the elbow and shake her, pushing his thin, wild-dog face close to hers, saying something which made her shake her head and try to back off.

Lendlova kept a firm hold of her arm. He went on talking at her. 'Take this!' he seemed to be saying. 'Go on, take it!'

There was something in his free hand; a small plastic envelope, the kind you might store pills or powder in.

Lola didn't want it. She tried to break free.

But Uncle Tomas went right on shoving the small package into her face until in the end she sagged some

23

more and let him slip it into her shirt pocket. He jabbed his finger at her; warning, threatening? Your guess is as good as mine.

She was crying for sure by this time.

And Lendlova pushed her against the locker and walked off at a hungry lope, right past me jammed in against the classroom door, throwing me a filthy look, but too contemptuous to pay an anonymous kid in a corridor more than a split second's attention.

He went round the corner and out of the building.

When I looked again, Lola had made it to the rest-room at last. I saw the door swing shut. I waited five minutes but she didn't come out.

By this time, the crowd was leaving the arena and drifting off home. The two basketball teams were filing down the corridor to the locker-room. Kate was coming down the corridor to find me, to show me a small piece on the back sports page of the Fortune City Times, which said that the first round draw for the Flushing Meadow Tournament beginning Monday had been drawn earlier that day.

'So?' I said, still looking out for Lola.

'So, read it!' Kate insisted.

' "Local girl, Lola Kodak, is drawn against number two seed, the current French number one, Bernice Matthieu," ' I read. ' "Pundits expect a close match. However, insiders have cast doubt on Kodak's match-fitness, and bookmakers indicate current odds of 2:1 in favour of Matthieu." '

I glanced up at Kate. 'That sucks.'

Kate nodded. 'Yeah. Being told by everyone that you're gonna lose can't do a whole lot for your confidence. Poor Lola.'

Poor Lola. My mind flashed back to Lendlova and the small plastic bag; the tears, the attempt to break free.

That was the part that really worried me. Lola and Lendlova, the coach from hell. How far would he push her?

3

'What Makes Lola Tick?'

Angel had hit upon this as the title for her documentary. It was due for broadcast on Tuesday, the day after the start of the American Open.

I'd spent the whole of Sunday with my dad at Heaven's Gate, pumping up the enigma side of Lola's personality. We had clips of her whacking the ball straight at her opponent, her expression stony and fixed. Shots of her receiving a glittering prize, holding it up to the crowd without the shadow of a smile. Film had been taken of her meeting the British royals at a gala event, of her shaking hands with the wife of the president of the United States.

And on not one of these occasions did the camera capture any reaction from Lola. Oh, and it goes without saying that Tomas Lendlova was always there too, equally expressionless, about eighteen inches behind her left shoulder, like some lean, wary bodyguard checking out possible assassins.

* * *

By Monday, when the tennis began, Carter and I weren't talking.

This is how it happened.

Lola was staying at Carter's house in Marytown; as the whole world knew.

Angel realises that Carter and I hang out together. Being the type to seize any opportunity, come Sunday, the day after the ball game, she put some pressure on me to fix up an interview for her with the 'welfare' family on Twenty-second Street. 'Nice angle!' she tells my dad.

I refused. I said I couldn't trade on the fact that I knew Joey to get her through a door that was closed to every other journalist in America. The Carters had made it clear that they wanted to protect Lola's privacy during the time she stayed at their house.

But Angel doesn't understand the word, 'No'. And a small lie here and there makes no difference to her. She went ahead and called their number anyway. She told Mrs Carter that I was due to call round to see Joey that evening, and would it be OK if I brought a sound recordist from Angelworks along with me; oh and maybe a small cameraman? No one would notice, they would fade into the wallpaper etcetera etcetera.

You can imagine. Joey's mom said no and told Joey. Joey obviously thought I should have put up more of a fight against Angel myself. So by the time we came to be sitting side by side on Court Number One, though the temperature was in the high eighties, the atmosphere between us was icy.

How come we had tickets to Flushing Meadow? That was down to my dad. As part of the documentary deal, Angelworks had been issued with a dozen free-passes. Sending one to Carter was Dad's way of overcoming the small local difficulty which he knew had developed between us.

And even Joey Carter doesn't have so much pride as to turn down a couple of days out of school watching a premier sporting event from a ringside seat.

We flew out Sunday evening, got fixed up with hotel rooms, spent the whole of Monday wandering around the Flushing Meadow ground, catching glimpses of Sampras, Courier, Hingis . . . and deliberately avoiding each other.

Easy to do. The place was packed. I saw the number five Men's seed go down in straight sets to an unknown player. Major upset. I saw a couple of tantrums from a fading star of a few years back. Not on the McEnroe 'You cannot be serious!' scale; no racket throwing, but plenty of bad language over a foot-fault call. It wrecked his concentration and he lost the match without winning another game.

Now and then, during the day, I would spot Joey in the distance. I smiled; he made out he didn't see.

'Enough!' I said when I finally cornered him on the way into Number One Court for the Matthieu-Kodak game. This is what the whole day had been building towards. 'It wasn't down to me that Angel made that phone call, OK!'

Carter shuffled up the stairs ahead of me in the bright sunlight. 'She said it was your idea.'

'Yeah, and you believed that!'

'. . . Anyway. This whole film thing; it sucks!' He sidled along the row to his seat, stepping on people's toes.

'. . . Meaning?'

'Meaning that just because a girl plays tennis, does she have to have people like Angel on her back, looking into every detail of her life? Like, what breakfast cereal does she eat? Where does she shop for underwear? Why doesn't she smile when they point the camera at her? . . . Don't they know her feelings are private property, period?'

I sat down next to him. 'Yeah,' I agreed.

He looked at me then with those deep blue eyes screwed up. 'Yeah?'

'Yeah. What can I do? I'm not Angel's keeper.'

He shrugged and grinned. We were cool again.

29

Now for the tennis.

The match between Lola and Bernice Matthieu was scheduled to begin at five-thirty, so I had five minutes to study the programme.

I read that Matthieu had been at the top of the Women's game for six years. She was five eight and weighed a hundred and forty pounds. Her picture showed a perfect athlete's body; compact, well-muscled, lithe. The white tennis gear showed off an all-year tan, the blonde streaks in her short, fair hair could have been natural or dyed in, I couldn't tell. Her record for the past twelve months read two Grand Slam championships and one runner-up.

Five-thirty arrived. But not the players. The crowd around us leaned forward to stare expectantly at the players' entrance. The hot sun baked the red clay court.

Five-thirty-five and a sprinkling of slow hand-clapping began. The umpire was sitting in his high seat, the people on line-duty had gathered nearby.

Carter and I glanced at each other. He shrugged.

I used the programme to fan my face, saw a movement beyond the screen blocking the players' dressing-room. 'Here they come!' I breathed.

Well, anyway, here Matthieu came. She marched on court solo, carrying her bag of rackets, without acknowledging the crowd. She looked moody and nervous. Upset.

Weird. The two players always walked out together. That was the sporting tradition.

'Lo-la . . . Lo-la . . . Lo-la!' the crowd began to chant.

'Where is she?' I hissed at Carter, as if he would have the answer.

'What can I tell you? She left our place before I did yesterday evening. Marcie was gonna drive her to the airport, but Lendlova showed up and did it instead. That's all I know!'

'Lo-la! . . . Lo-la!'

Matthieu dumped her bag by the umpire's chair and unzipped her top.

I stared at the players' entrance.

'She always shows up late,' someone nearby said. 'She does it to get under her opponent's skin.'

It seemed to be working. I noticed Matthieu begin to pace up and down the side of the court.

'. . . No, there's a problem,' someone else said, pointing at the entrance.

More movement there. But it was Tomas Lendlova, not Lola, who showed up on court.

The chanting and slow clapping stopped. The whole stadium fell quiet.

Lola's coach walked slowly to the umpire's chair. He stood on tiptoe and reached to cover the guy's microphone with his hand before he spoke a few words.

Silence on the court. Ten thousand eyes bored into Lendlova.

He finished what he had to say, turned and left.

'Ladies and gentlemen,' the umpire announced.

You could have heard a pin drop. I don't know how else to say that. I mean, that kind of hush from that number of people . . .

'Ladies and gentlemen, I regret to inform you that Lola Kodak is injured and has retired from the competition.'

Stunned silence. Then uproar. I remember Bernice Matthieu standing in the middle of a knot of officials, looking kind of stranded before they hustled her off.

The umpire got down from his chair. The crowd stood up and started to boo. Sympathy is not what you get when you disappoint ten thousand people who paid good money to watch a closely-fought competition. It was to have been the last match of the day, a chance to get patriotic and yell for your girl to beat the Frenchwoman against the odds.

I could see the bank of journalists squatting courtside get out their cellular phones and start jabbering to their editors. TV cameras rolled, announcers told the nation the astounding fact that Lola Kodak had failed to show up for the American Open; news that would knock a hurricane in Tennessee off the top slot.

Oh, and I noticed Angel Christian panicking about her documentary. Lola Kodak without Lola. 'Hamlet' without the prince.

'Let's go!' I said to Carter.

The crowd was breaking up and leaking out of the stadium, there was room to squeeze down to the front and listen in on what Angel was saying to my dad.

'How could she do this?' she was yelling, taking it personally. 'We're set up to film her snatching victory, we're giving her fifteen million viewers, and what happens? Her ankle hurts, she has a touch of muscle spasm, so she pulls out of the whole shooting-match!'

Angel's mother was Italian, so Angel's given to melodramatic outbursts. She speaks with her hands, throwing out gestures like physical blows.

'Well, great! Fine! Just don't ask me to make another documentary on an overpaid, jumped-up little kid from the back streets of Fortune City!'

'Angel!' Dad waited for a nano-second gap. 'This could be good.'

She withered him with a scornful look. 'Yeah, sure. The subject of our film pulls out of a major competition. We have nothing to film. That's real good!'

'Wait. Do we believe this injured ankle story?' Dad appealed to the rest of the crew and me and Carter.

We shook our heads.

'So what's the real reason?'

More head shaking, some shrugs.

'Are we surprised she's done it?'

Weird question, Dad. But it made Angel stop and think.

'You know, Sean, you're right!' Her face lit up. That's the Italian thing too; the sudden switch from angry to excited. 'We are *not* surprised she failed to show up. And the reason is, these last few days Lola's been behaving pretty strangely, hiding herself away, maybe building to some sort of crisis . . .'

I turned to Carter to see if he agreed.

Angel was on a roll. 'It's obvious when you think about it. All the signs were there that she was on her way to a major crack-up – this Garbo thing of wanting to be alone.'

Dad knew he didn't have to say any more. He stepped back, ducked his head in a little, satisfied gesture.

I admire my dad. Did I say that? He has good looks, good judgement and a small ego. His sentences are never littered unnecessarily with the word 'I'.

Angel formed a plan. She would take her crew into

34

the players' changing-room and film the final sequence of her documentary standing next to Lola Kodak's empty locker. She would speak straight to camera, raising a giant question mark over the Golden Girl's future.

'Let's go, guys!' she said, springing into action as the crowd finally trickled from the stadium.

That was when Carter held me back and told me quickly about what he'd seen behind the scenes after the schools basketball final – Lola breaking down in tears, her uncle pushing her about, handing over a packet that looked like tablets of some kind.

I gasped. 'What are you saying?'

'Nothing for definite. Only that she broke down. I don't know the reason. And that Lendlova didn't give a damn.'

'But what about the plastic envelope? Are you saying it was drugs?' The idea shot like an arrow into the front of my brain. Pills. Banned substances. Performance-enhancing drugs. The implications were enormous.

Carter frowned and shook his head. 'I don't know. OK?'

'Not OK. Why didn't you say something? Joey, this could be . . . wow, it could be . . . huge!'

Suppose Lendlova had been forcing illegal drugs on to Lola to improve her chances of beating Matthieu?

Say she'd resisted. She would have been scared of the random tests, of being caught. Who wouldn't? She'd say no to taking them; her uncle would insist with that wolf-look of his. He'd stay right there until she swallowed them down.

Lola would have had Sunday to sweat and grow even more afraid. By today, five-thirty and the moment of truth, with the drugs still in her system, her nerve would have given way. So she'd invented a last-minute reason and pulled out.

'Carter?' I was too caught up in my idea at first to realise that he wasn't responding.

Then I turned to follow the direction of his gaze across the Centre Court towards the box where the family and friends of the competitors sit. There was a low sun sending deep, dark shadows across the red court, highlighting the bank of yellow and purple flowers beneath the box. For a few seconds I had to wait for my eyes to adjust to the glare.

Carter was watching three people in the box. One of them was Tomas Lendlova, who had his back to us and was speaking to a middle-aged, well-heeled looking couple. I had them down straight away as Lola's parents, Dr and Mrs Kodak.

And let's say that the discussion up there was animated. Lendlova was doing his finger-jabbing thing.

Lola's father took it for a while, then pushed him off. Mrs Kodak tried to get in between the two of them. She looked like an older version of her daughter; hair a couple of shades darker, cut in a bob, but the same pale, oval face and wide grey eyes. There was no resemblance whatsoever between her and her wolf-brother.

Anyway, he jabbed, Dr Kodak pushed, Mrs Kodak wedged herself in between. Then Lendlova must have sworn or got the final word in some way, because the couple backed off. She sat down weakly in a chair. He stood there stunned as the brother slammed out of the box.

'So here we are, Day One of the Open Championship with high hopes resting on the number one girl of American tennis!' Angel Christian looked earnestly into camera, a neat mike tucked into the lapel of her primrose-yellow suit.

Dax the cameramen went in close, picking up Angel's face and the grey metal locker behind. The door was open, a stack of rackets piled on a shelf.

Carter and I had made our way from the court in time to see Angel doing her closing piece for tomorrow's programme.

'The number one girl who has it all!' Angel went on.

'Lola Kodak's meteoric rise has given her millions of dollars worth of prize money and even more in sponsorship deals. Her name is on the sportswear that you and I buy, she's backed by a big German car company, she advertises everything from high energy drinks to soap powder on TV.'

We know all this, so get to the point, I thought.

'And yet . . .' Angel said, giving it the dramatic pause. '. . . What we see when we get up close is a girl under pressure. We see relentless training, endless travelling, the hopping from hotel room to hotel room across the world. And then we see the stress of competing. Never relaxing, always striving to be the best.'

Dad made a motion for her to hurry it up.

Angel's gaze didn't flicker. 'And now,' she said, pulling it round to her final point, 'the inevitable has happened. A crack has opened and threatens to swallow her.'

Don't push it, I wanted to say; *the girl has only pulled out of one tennis match. Hardly a tragedy*. Not knowing what Angel had in reserve until the moment she put it on tape.

'At the time of talking to you, six-thirty on Monday evening, we just have news through that will shock the whole sports world.' Angel's voice tightened, grew tense. Dax went in closer still. 'Early reports that Lola had pulled out of the championship due to an ankle injury have quickly proved unfounded. A newsflash leaked to NBC and broadcast ten minutes ago gives a different story.'

I curled my hands into tight fists, as if clenching them would make any difference to what I was hearing. I noticed Carter screw up his eyes in disbelief.

'The fact is, Lola has no injury, no physical reason why she could not have played this match. She sent no message, gave no explanation to her coach, Tomas Lendlova. A major mystery has developed; the police are involved. Big questions with, as yet, no answers. All we know for sure is that Lola Kodak has vanished!'

4

Crack . . . cracked . . . crack-up . . . crack cocaine. Boy, one word can carry a whole lot of baggage.

Think about it. Craziness, burn-out, breakdown, overdose. All these things bounced around in my head on the plane back to Fortune City.

Angel talked about a big crack opening up in Lola Kodak's perfect world. She mentioned pressure and the fact that no one knew what was going on behind the girl's mask-like expression. Meltdown.

This was the favoured theory; that Lola had somehow pressed the self-destruct button on the world of Mercedes and million dollar contracts.

As yet, no one had hit on the crooked-coach line of inquiry. But then, Kate was the only person I'd mentioned the plastic package to. I mean, you can't exactly go around accusing a guy of high crimes and misdemeanours on account of the fact that you don't like the shape of his face and one small, possibly innocent envelope.

However, it was our favoured option; Kate's and mine. 'Did you see Lendlova's face when the umpire gave the match to Matthieu?' I asked her as we came in to land late on Tuesday afternoon. We'd cut short our trip. Somehow the tennis at Flushing Meadow seemed to have lost its attraction.

'Homicidal!' she agreed. 'I was afraid he was going to mow down the ball-girl in a hail of invisible bullets.'

'And how come he waited until the last possible minute before he told anyone that his player hadn't shown up?' I was hazy about this part, but it must have been obvious to the coach that his player wasn't in the locker-room before the match. Yet he'd let it go right to the line.

'You mean, that kind of shows he was implicated?' Kate considered the possibility. 'If he wasn't involved in Lola's disappearance, he would've raised the alarm sooner?'

'I guess.' The kind of guilt we were talking about was still the supplying of illegal drugs kind. I didn't suspect anything more direct, like kidnap. I mean, what would be the point?

The plane tilted to one side and circled the runway. The wing flaps jerked down and the engines choked back ready for landing. One thump and we melted rubber on to tarmac.

'So what do we do?' Kate asked as we came through the Arrivals gate. 'We can't just do nothing!'

'Let me check with Marcie.' I wanted to go through

what had happened when Uncle Tomas came to our place to pick up his niece to take her to the airport on Sunday evening. This wasn't going to take too long, since we'd arranged for my sister to drive us home, and there she was now, standing by the barrier in her long, printed skirt, sandals and braided hair. Don't get me wrong; tomorrow the hippy gear could be gone and she'd be wearing leather. With Marcie you never could tell.

'OK,' she said wearily as we inhaled emission fumes sitting in gridlock on State Hill. It was Tuesday afternoon rush-hour. A million computer programmers had logged off and headed for home. 'I'll give it to you one more time.'

'Go ahead.' I was in the back seat. Kate was sitting up front.

'Lola had a time for Tomas to pick her up. Six pm. He'd arranged to drive his car down the side of the block, park in the area where we keep the trash cans and slip in the back way without being noticed. She made a point of being packed and ready half an hour early, said he didn't like to be kept waiting.' Marcie tapped the steering-wheel with her plum-coloured, pointed fingernails.

'Did she seem uptight?' Kate asked.

I couldn't see Marcie's face, but I heard a little 'Huh!' and an unfunny laugh. 'When was Lola *not* uptight?'

'But more than usual?' Kate hung on in.

'Well, maybe. But I put that down to the big match the next day.' The traffic moved nine and a half feet, then stopped. 'And I got the impression that she'd had it up to here with training and travelling. She actually said she envied me my life, just sitting round playing music, hanging out!' This time the laugh was genuine.

'So what happened when Tomas showed up?' I asked.

'Hmm.' Marcie thought hard. 'I can only describe it as shutters coming up, or a light being switched off. No more off-guard moments, no girly giggles. No hugs when we said goodbye.'

'Is she scared of him?' was Kate's question.

'No, that's too strong. She doesn't like him, though. You can tell by body language and stuff. I'd say she resented him; a bit like a gaoler coming to lock you up. You know it's his job, but you blame him for choosing it in the first place. Anyway, I got a stiff thanks and goodbye, then Tomas grabbed her bag and stampeded her out of the back basement exit, up the fire-escape into the yard and away before the pressmen caught on.'

We sat for a while as the line of cars eased and Marcie turned north for Twenty-second Street. 'You know she never made it to her hotel?' I reminded Marcie. This was a detail I'd picked up from the news bulletins.

Silence. Worried silence. More essence of exhaust.

Kate and I shared our anxieties over Uncle Tomas. 'What do you think?' we said. Marcie said she still thought it was self-destruct. Lola always had that tendency behind the blank look; a grain of craziness, recklessness, the possibility that one day she could throw it all away.

'When you know someone as well as I knew Lola, you get a feeling that you don't put into words. And yeah, this could be the moment. It wouldn't surprise me. But hey, she'll turn up.' Marcie tried to reassure herself. 'She'll think of the money and bite the bullet. The girl would have to be insane not to!'

I hadn't expected the cops to be buzzing around number 342; a car, a uniform at the door, an FBI woman inside the house. Pastrami-on-rye man, eat your heart out.

They let me and Marcie into our own home, but sent Kate away.

'Call me,' she said.

I'd waited months to hear that from her, but not in the present context of a gun in a holster, a cop's beady eye. The 'Call me' I wanted was softer, there would be mood music, she'd be wearing the white top with the narrow black band around a V-neck that I liked, her hair would be loose . . . yeah.

'Carter, call me!' she insisted as I disappeared on the arm of Sergeant Kopalski.

So I won't go through the questions the cops asked, since they were more or less a repeat of what Kate and I had squeezed out of Marcie. It struck me again that somewhere between number 342 Twenty-second Street and the Radisson Hotel at Flushing Meadow, Lendlova had committed the unbelievably careless act of losing Lola Kodak.

So I told the detective the one piece of solid information that I thought might have a bearing, concerning the plastic envelope.

She listened but gave nothing away. 'Thanks, Joey,' she said. She chewed her lip, one eye on the TV, where Bernice Matthieu was powering her way through to a second round victory.

Forty-love, four games to three, second set; first set to Matthieu.

'I can tell you, however, that Lendlova isn't top of our list,' Detective Starkweather confided. She was kind of thinking aloud. 'You wouldn't believe the bunch of losers and no-hopers, drifters and whackos that hang round a girl like Lola.'

'Such as?' I asked. This was the first time this had crossed my mind.

The detective wasn't a Cagney and Lacey or NYPD Blues type. I mean, she missed out on the glamour stakes.

She looked more like my mom if you want to know; short curly brown hair, a little overweight. And she liked to talk. 'You've heard of guys who stalk the rich and famous, haven't you? Jodie Foster had one years ago. So did Monica Seles. Usually they're harmless, but once in a while they can blow up and do something stupid.'

'You don't say.' (Necessary to mutter something just to oil the wheels).

'Then you get an Angel Christian situation on your hands.' Starkweather reminded us all of the recent stalker drama that had happened much closer to home. Then she turned her attention to the TV. Matthieu had just stormed to victory. There was an interview for the sport channel.

Hey, I realised, the detective was talking kidnap, assault and murder here! She was saying they thought Lola was a victim of some lunatic lurking in the tramlines of her career.

'. . . Lauren played well in the first set, but when I broke serve in the second, I knew I could take the match,' Matthieu said in a heavy French accent. She accepted the interviewer's congratulations, then jerked the subject away from her current triumph.

'I need . . . I want to say something about my friend and doubles partner, Lola Kodak.'

We all sat up then; me, Marcie, my mom hovering in the background, and especially Detective Starkweather.

Me, partly because this was the first I'd heard about Lola playing any games of doubles with the Frenchwoman.

'Go ahead.' The interviewer stood to one side.

'Lola!' Bernice said it directly to the camera, her face shiny with sweat from the match, her blonde hair wet and plastered to her head. 'If you're watching this, wherever you are, we wish you to make contact! Please. If there's a problem, come and tell us. Don't stay in hiding, come forward to speak to someone.' She stammered over a couple of words, then stumbled to a halt in what looked like a very moving and genuine appeal.

'Hmm.' Starkweather grunted. She turned to the uniformed cop at the door. 'Did you see that guy in the crowd behind Matthieu?'

He shrugged. There had been a dozen guys in shot.

'The one with the round shades and goatee beard. Did you recognise him?' The detective could be very sharp and focused when necessary. I'd only vaguely taken in the sea of faces behind the French player.

When the other cop shook his head, Starkweather pounced. 'Matthew King!' she snapped. 'Longtime stalker of women tennis players. Transferred his attention from Sabatini when she retired a few years back. Has been through a couple more since then, including the Williams sisters. Currently obsessed with, guess who?'

'Lola Kodak,' we murmured. It came across as a little ripple of whispers.

'Right. Matthew King. 29 years old, unemployed, college drop-out. Seen in Fortune City last weekend, hanging around outside this very house.'

They crawl out from under stones, these creeps. They hang around your door and you don't even know it. I shuddered like it was cold, when really we were having a heatwave out there.

'I'm on to it,' the sergeant said, taking out his radio and barking instructions to his buddies down at section headquarters.

I'd called Kate to bring her up to speed and settled down to watch 'What Makes Lola Tick?', updated to include the latest bulletin on the disappearance. There was only me in the house; everyone else had had enough excitement and gone across to my pa's cousin's house to chill out.

I was waiting for Kate to come round to talk through this latest Matthew King thing.

Angel was up to the part in the programme where she was probing the motivation of a kid like Lola to work and work until she made it to the top. Was it that some people were born more ambitious than others? (Angel should know the answer to that!) Or was it that Lola was more susceptible to pressure from the outside (i.e. from dear old Uncle Tomas).

Then I heard a noise down in the basement.

Or maybe not. I chose to carry on listening to Angel.

She laid it on the line; the fact that fanaticism, obsession, a kind of brutal single-mindedness were essential ingredients of the top tennis star's make-up.

To my mind, Lola didn't fit the picture. She'd lived at my house for the weekend. She'd eaten ice-cream with my sister. I'd seen her in pyjamas at breakfast looking about twelve years old.

There it was again; a noise, a door opening in the basement. This time I couldn't ignore it.

'Hey!' I went into the hall and called down the stairs. 'Who's there?'

You don't know how you'll act in these situations until they happen. I might have been thinking, 'Who left the goddam door open for all the neighbourhood stray dogs to wander into the house?'

A figure burst up the stair-well two at a time. A guy coming at me with raised fists, knocking me back against the bannister, pinning me there with his forearm across my throat.

Oh Jesus, Tomas Lendlova!

He squeezed my Adam's apple, throttled the life out of me. I could see every inch of dark stubble on that long, lean jaw, the glint of his brown, hooded eyes.

'What did you tell the cops?' he snarled.

'Nothing!' I lied. 'Believe me; nothing!'

He didn't. Instead, he increased the pressure on my throat and said he would kill me, shoot me dead, stab me through the heart if it turned out I'd uttered one single word about the small, see-through plastic envelope which he'd handed to Lola on Saturday night.

5

So Lola had a stalker. Fact. There was a guy out there obsessed with every move she made.

Question: Did stalkers exist before radio, TV and cinema were invented?

This was something to think about as I made my way across town to Joey's place. I mean, before actors, rock stars and sports players got real famous and had their lives plastered across *People* magazine, who would be bothered to hang around outside their doors? Who, pre-*People*, would have fantasised that the star might one day look to earth and notice little, crazy Joe Soap, the insignificant speck in the crowd?

What I'm saying is, what price fame? I mean, Angel had only just survived Brett-Crazy-Guy-Roberts.

If stalkers and obsessives and seriously weird guys are part of it, you can keep it.

The cops had named one Matthew King. He was known to them. He was there at Flushing Meadow. It was all looking like a case of kidnap or worse. Which meant that Carter and I had been way off-target when we suspected Lendlova. The small plastic packet had misled us.

Only, there were still a couple of things I wanted to talk through. Like, the coach's behaviour between Lola going AWOL and the start of the match against Matthieu. To my mind, that looked like a suspicious silence. And the angry discussion between Lendlova and the Kodaks in the stadium; what had that been about?

Which is why, on a fine Tuesday evening, I had decided to skip 'What Makes Lola Tick?' on TV and head for Twenty-second Street.

I'm not saying that an excuse to spend time with Carter wasn't part of it too. In fact, I was hoping to find the house empty except for him, since Joey had mentioned the fact that his entire family was out for the evening; information carefully inserted into his phone call to me about Weirdo King.

I was pleased he'd mentioned it, working out his motive as I walked past the deli at the top of the block, telling myself that it was Joey's way of inviting me over to get up-close and personal. I mean, why would he say the house was empty otherwise? Or was I reading too much into an innocent remark? In which case, I was regretting changing into my white V-neck top which I know he likes. In which case, should I think about turning round and going right back home?

A gang of kids gathered by the wire fence of an empty parking-lot and watched me walk. They wore T-shirts covered in the names of bands, cartoon characters and one that read 'Don't Trust Anyone Below 14,000 Feet'. Hmm. One kid bounced a basketball, *thud-thud* on to the asphalt. One hooked his fingers through the chain links and followed my every move.

So I headed right on to number 342, wishing the white top wasn't so tight, refusing to let those kids see that their stares bothered me.

Knock-knock at Carter's door. No reply.

'It's Carter's woman!' the boy with the basketball yelled.

I won't tell you what else they implied. By this time I'd lost it. I came back down the steps and round the side of the house, down the alleyway and into the yard with the trash-cans. The yard was actually a small, damp, dirty gap between two high-rise blocks with the short row of brownstone houses wedged in between. There was just enough room between the heaped-up trash for one car to be parked there, partly blocking my way. Not pretty. But there was a back door into Joey's basement and I planned to use it.

So I was out of sight of the monkeys in the chain-link compound, my heart was already pumping too fast and I was regretting everything when I took the steps down to Carter's basement.

'. . . You keep your mouth shut, or else!'

I heard a voice in the hall above, then a couple of thuds. I was slow to react. I thought, 'This is some kind of joke!'

'. . . If you go to the cops, you're dead meat!'

Lendlova? Talking to Carter? Rather, yelling, snarling, growling at Carter.

I didn't hear a reply, which worried me.

I froze where I was, three steps out of the basement. Find something heavy to smack the guy over the head with, I told myself, retreating into Marcie's studio and looking round for a metal microphone stand, a stool; anything. Maybe I should've been thinking about calling the cops instead, who knows?

I was wasting time searching for a suitable blunt instrument when Carter must have made his break. There was some shoving and pushing, which must mean that Lendlova's threats weren't backed up with a gun or a knife; otherwise Joey wouldn't have risked making a move.

But his chances of winning a fist fight against the tennis coach weren't great, I reckoned. Lendlova must have been fifty, but as an ex-professional sportsman he was still more dangerous than most twenty year olds. Carter was fit, but he wasn't big. That's why the thuds and the sound of fists hitting bone from up above scared the hell out of me.

I grabbed a metal chair and took the steps two at a time. In the hall, Joey was up against the bannister, blood trickling from his mouth, his feet kicking out at Lendlova, who was piling in with more punches.

Lifting the chair, I smacked it down on Tomas's shoulders and head.

Carter ducked sideways as Lendlova crashed forwards; more out of surprise than because I'd hit him hard. It gave us a couple of seconds; no more.

'This way!' I grabbed Joey's arm and pulled him down the steps.

He was dazed, off-balance, stumbling into me, so we both ended up on the floor in the basement.

And Lendlova had got it back together, was coming after us.

'Let's get out!' Dragging Carter again, thinking we had more chance out in the open, I made it to the door, up the steps into the yard.

I'll never forget the wild look on Lendlova's face, the glaring eyes, the curled lip and too many teeth showing as he leaped out of the basement. It looked like he wanted to rip us both apart.

I turned in the tight space and crashed against a trash-can, tipping it over the hood of the parked car; plastic packaging, bottles, paper everywhere. Metal crunched and scraped, clattered and echoed.

Carter went one way around the car, I went the other. Lendlova jumped right up on to the hood to cut us both off.

He stood poised, ready to pounce as we scrambled through the cardboard cartons and empty beer cans.

And then there was a sharp, sudden bang and the guy crumpled. He hunched up, hugging his chest, sagging forwards until he toppled from the car on to the ground.

Nothing made sense. It was crazy.

I made some kind of gasping sound and half-crawled towards the man on the floor. Carter scrabbled through the trash to find him and turn him over.

Lendlova groaned. His eyes were open, his face like a mask.

Joey eased the coach's hands away from his chest to see how much blood we were dealing with.

Too much. It had soaked through his zip-up top and was pumping out. He was looking at us as if we were a long way off.

'Don't move him!' I warned. Instinct made me glance up in the direction of the shot; there were twenty storeys of blank windows in the block opposite, a gunman in one of them. 'We need an ambulance! Joey, we need help!'

'Listen!' Lendlova tried to speak. He reached out to catch hold of my hand.

I wanted to pull it away, to get free, but he wouldn't let me.

'No time,' he groaned. 'Listen, listen!'

Joey tried to lift his head and slide a padding of cardboard packaging under it. We both backed off from touching the wound in his chest.

'Lola!' he whispered.

'Where is she?' To me it seemed like this was the one last, desperate thing Lendlova needed to tell us.

'Oh God!' His voice was fainter, his eyelids were fluttering closed over those amber-brown wolf-eyes. 'Listen, she ran out on me on Sunday night. I pulled in for gas, she went to the rest-room. I never saw her again . . .'

I couldn't bear to look at Lendlova. I kept my eyes fixed on Joey, who was still trying to make the guy more comfortable.

'So where is she now?' Joey asked.

'. . . Don't know. They got to her.'

'Who? Who got to Lola?'

'She made a run for it, but they took her anyway.'

'Man, who are we talking about?' Carter leaned forward so he could catch what Lendlova was saying.

'Matthew!' he whispered.

I could hardly hear. The breath was noisy, catching in his throat, blocking what he said with his dying gasp. I felt him release his grip on me.

'Matthew. Game, set and match!' he said. Tennis metaphor; his last little joke. His eyes closed. That was it.

'Kate, are you OK?'

Carter and I had stumbled out of the yard, back into the house. I didn't know where I was, or who was holding me, asking me how I was.

'Kate, speak to me! I called the cops. Hang on, they'll be here!'

It was Joey looking after me, putting his arms around me, letting me hold on to him and take in gulps of air until I could stop crying and shaking, until the nightmare receded.

'He's dead!' I sobbed. 'Someone shot him. God, Joey, what's going on?'

'And you're sure that's what he said?' Detective Starkweather turned from me to Joey and back again.

She'd showed up with the uniformed cops and

paramedics, who had pronounced Tomas Lendlova dead at the scene. The forensic guys were out in the yard at this very moment, erecting a screen, taking pictures of the body, letting the pathologist get to work.

'He said they took Lola after she tried to run away from him on Sunday night.' Those words were etched in my brain. 'And that Matthew was responsible.' Game, set and match.

'Did he say Matthew who?' The detective was very laid back, sitting backwards way around on a chair in Joey's kitchen, legs straddling the seat, leaning her arms along the back rim. The only thing about her that said 'cop' was the gun in the holster fitting snugly under her arm.

I checked with Joey then shook my head. 'It was difficult to hear, but I don't remember a surname. He did use the word "they" . . . "*They* got to her . . . *they* took her anyway".'

'Meaning more than one person was involved in the abduction.' Detective Starkweather made a mental note. 'And could you tell my ballistics guys anything about the direction of the gunshot?'

Taking a deep breath, I relived the moment when Lendlova had clutched at his chest and crumpled forward from the hood of the car. 'I'd say it came from a window fairly high up in the block opposite.'

Carter nodded in agreement. 'Won't they get that from the angle of the bullet?'

Starkweather shrugged. 'Maybe. But it looks like the bullet passed right through. And it made quite a mess in transit.'

I winced and she laid off. 'Sorry, Kate. Listen, if you think of anything else that could be useful, you let me know, OK?'

She stood up then and checked her watch. 'When do you expect your folks to get back?' she asked Carter.

'Pretty soon. I called them just after I called you. They said they'd be here soon as they could.'

'And your dad?' The detective turned to check on me one last time.

'Likewise.' I could feel myself still shaking, my mind full of jagged, violent fragments that kept pushing themselves to the surface.

'You take care, OK.' She nodded at me as a uniformed cop came into the room to mutter something in her ear. 'Listen, they searched the building opposite from top to bottom; there's no gunman there now, you hear?'

Carter was as dazed as me as we both stared back at her.

'What I'm saying is, there's no immediate danger that he or she will take another shot at potential witnesses. It should be quite safe for you to go about your business as normal.'

'What about you? What's your next move?' Carter was the one who got it together to ask.

'After we clean up out here?' She sounded and looked like the housekeeper, except we were talking bleeding bodies not dirty linen. 'We move fast on the Matthew thing, since it's the best lead we've got.'

'Matthew King?' Carter keeps a clearer head than me at times. Mostly I'm methodical and logical as the next person, but not when there's blood around.

'Sure, Matthew King. Who else?'

Starkweather made it absolutely clear that Lola's stalker was the guy they were after. They'd close in on him somewhere here in Fortune City, or failing that, put the cops at Flushing Meadow on standby in case he made his way back there.

'You think he's holding Lola prisoner?' Carter wanted to know. He followed the detective down the steps into the basement.

This time she didn't give him an answer.

Meaning, she thought King might be holding his victim in some secret place, or else he'd already killed her. Either way was grim.

I hate those meaningful silences.

I got gunshots inside my head again, blood on the brain.

But, as Joey said after the policewoman had made her exit into the yard to talk to Forensics: 'Why shoot Lendlova? And one other thing; don't weirdo stalkers usually act alone?'

So who was the 'they' Tomas had mentioned? Maybe Detective Starkweather was thinking this through as she lifted the flap in the white plastic screen, ducked her head and went through to take a look at the body and listen to stuff about the trajectory of the bullet, the type of gun, and whether or not the murderer would have used telescopic sights to line up his victim before he fired.

6

Wednesday morning I went to school like nothing had happened.

I didn't think Kate would make it, so I was surprised to see her standing by the lockers with Connie and Zoey. I mean, I'd never seen her in pieces the way she was over the shooting, so I expected her to at least take time out from school.

Not that I'd had much sleep either. When it's all over and you're alone in your room, staring at the cracks in the ceiling, there's nothing to come between you and your worst fears. Like, what if the gunman had missed and hit me or Kate by mistake? Like, maybe we could have done more to save Lendlova once he'd been shot. I need First Aid classes, I need my guts not to tie themselves up and my hands not to shake at the sight of blood.

For the first time in my life I knew first-hand the meaning of Post-Traumatic Stress Disorder. Action replay over and over, the pause button stuck on that frame where the shot was fired, Lendlova hugging himself and keeling forward.

But I said hi to Zig at the gate and walked into the school building. 'Hey!' I said to kids who hadn't listened to the news and knew zilch about the killing. 'Yeah, the tennis was great, thanks.' Sampras got knocked out, but Venus Williams was storming through to meet Bernice Matthieu next round.

I saw in a flash that Kate wanted me not to mention the shooting; the way she greeted me and kept Zoey and Connie on either side as we all walked down the corridor to class. You have to block out a lot of the garbage to carry on as normal, and your friends can help you do that.

'Hey, Zig,' I said, 'did you see the latest de Caprio movie yet? How about we get a group together to go to the Multiplex this weekend?'

Beneath the surface, though, it was tough. Like, there's only so much of your mind that you can control; the outer layers. On the inside, the subconscious keeps on flinging things out. Matthew King's face in the crowd behind the Frenchwoman when she gave that interview. I'd say that was a pretty weird face, with the goatee beard and round glasses. I don't approve of facial hair, especially the sort that's neatly shaped and trimmed. I think it shows a warped personality. Like, too much attention to hair follicles. It's the same, only the opposite, when women pluck their eyebrows to the point when they hardly exist.

Vanity–insanity?

And King's glasses had glinted in the sun, hiding his eyes, but his whole attitude showed he was pleased to be in camera shot; a slack smile on his lips, a fixed stare at the lens instead of at Bernice.

But – and I spent the whole day thinking about this – guys like Matthew King – obsessives, psychopaths – they're loners. They live in their own sealed little worlds. They don't have helpers.

So, it didn't make sense to me that King was in Flushing Meadow on Tuesday, at the time when Bernice gave the interview pleading for Lola to get in touch. Logically he should have been holed up with his victim, gloating over her, making like she'd chosen to be kidnapped, she was having a great, intimate, one-to-one time and no way did he plan to do her even the slightest bit of harm.

'*Lola, Lola, you're mine, all mine!*'

'. . . Joey, can we meet after school?' Kate's voice cut into my thoughts as I ran through this for the twentieth time that day. We were in the corridor between Social Science and English. In the far distance, Miss Slay was garnering girls for the school tennis team. 'I need to talk!' Kate whispered.

'By the gate. We can walk home through the park,' I suggested.

'Kate Brennan, I need you to play in the team

65

tomorrow!' Slay trundled down the corridor towards us, squashing small people against walls. She wore an expression of noble suffering, like she was personally involved in Lola Kodak's tragedy but was determined to carry on with life. She even managed to give the impression that she held the key to the golden girl's disappearance, but that you mustn't press her to tell. *All this in a person's expression*, I hear you say. But, believe me, Slay can do it.

'Couldn't you leave me out of the team this one time?' Kate began.

I left her to plead, knowing who would come out tops. A thousand dollars on Slay.

'. . . I'm playing second couple,' Kate sighed when we met as planned.

'Let's walk.' I started up the sidewalk, past the school bus parked at the stop. 'Let's talk.'

'Are you OK?' Kate asked, first off.

We were clear of the knots of kids, walking under the track of the Loop train, between the fat concrete pillars. 'Lousy,' I admitted. 'You?'

'Lousy too. I know it's a cliché, but I keep expecting to wake up and find this is all a bad dream.'

'You want to know what I think?' When we reached the park and saw the green space, trees, the white monument on the hill, I felt the tension ease a little. 'I think we shouldn't fix all our attention on Matthew King.'

Kate said nothing for a while. There were the usual fat pigeons and skateboarders, the usual sad old bag-lady feeding corn to one and swearing at the others. 'Lendlova named him,' she reminded me.

'Yeah. But he could've been mistaken. And what if there's more than one thing going on here?' I flashed her a look. The sun made her hair shine lighter. I never knew a girl less conscious of the way she looks though. Like, I bet she doesn't spend more than five minutes per day looking in the mirror. No eyebrow tweezers. Did I say that when she cried in my arms the day before, she didn't wipe away the tears? And yet, no smudged mascara, no red nose.

'That's what I've been thinking,' she told me. 'Lendlova did tell us that Lola went to the rest-room at the gas station and took off without him. He didn't make it sound like it was a kidnap at that point.'

('Hey, you! You run that board at one more bird and I'll call the cops!' Kid on skateboard cruises by. Pigeon flaps and flutters. Bag-lady shakes her fist.)

'Exactly.' I tried to concentrate. There were a lot of distractions. 'You know Lola was partnering Bernice Matthieu in the Women's Doubles event?' Where did that come into it? I didn't know. It just came into my head.

('You hear me? I'll have you arrested!' Pigeon settles on bag-lady's raised fist and pecks for more corn. Skateboarder sails on down the hill.)

'She was, but she pulled out,' Kate told me.

'She did? How do you know that?'

'Angel found out from the organisers. I overheard her telling Dad. It probably isn't important.'

Players did that if they found their schedule of singles matches was too heavy. The prize money in doubles was lower, and there was less status in the event.

So we moved on. 'Let's say Lola had had it up to here. Let's even say that the pills in the plastic envelope thing is correct.' I meant that it was like we said; Lendlova had been pressurising Lola to take performance-enhancing drugs. His protegé had protested. She'd decided that the only thing to do was to get the hell out.

'So she ran before they reached the Radisson Hotel.' Kate was thinking along the same lines.

(*Mutter-mutter* from the bag-lady. Coos and pecks from the plump pigeon, until we left them to their harmless love affair.)

'And then something unexpected happened, which we don't know anything about!' I felt that tight, trapped feeling I'd had all day begin to ease. We were walking faster, up the hill to the monument, in amongst the fluttering flags. 'Listen, what we have to work out is why anyone would want to shoot Lendlova. Then my bet is we get closer to why Lola isn't putting in an appearance either.'

'OK.' Kate thought for a minute. 'Tomas Lendlova could have been part of some huge drugs conspiracy on the professional tennis circuit. He knew all the names involved; in fact he was part of it.'

I nodded and looked up at the flags: the Stars and Stripes; the Fortune City emblem, gold on blue.

'But something had gone wrong amongst the drugs suppliers. Maybe Lendlova had screwed up and was threatening to blow the whole thing open.'

'Name names? Bring down some of the top players and coaches?' I was getting enthusiastic about this idea. There's a lot of money in the international game. And where there are big prizes, you get some people crossing the border between legal and illegal ways of winning.

'Of course, we'd have to find proof . . .' Kate circled the monument and came back to where I stood.

Problem. Dead men don't give answers. And besides Tomas Lendlova's mysterious little packet, what else did we have to go on?

We were so busy trying to dig ourselves out of this one that we didn't notice the couple walking up Monument Hill towards us until they reached the statue.

'Joey Carter?' the woman asked.

I was still so shaken up that I jumped like someone had poked a gun in my back. When I turned and tried to place where I had seen these well-dressed people before, my mind was a blank.

The woman was dressed in a dark suit with knee-length skirt and high-heeled shoes. She wore a white blouse with a pointed collar. Her dark red hair was cut neat. He stood a little behind; grey-haired, serious to the point where he was frowning.

'Mrs Kodak?' Kate recognised the woman first and took half a step towards her.

'Yes.' She put up her hand; a polite warning for Kate to stay out of it. 'Joey, we watched you come out of school and followed you here. We need to talk to you about Lola.'

Behind the calm, careful explanation, Lola's mother was going through a lot. 'How did you know me?' I asked.

'We remember you from when you were a small boy. You haven't changed so much that we wouldn't recognise you.'

This was news to me, that the Kodaks knew anything about the Carters. Like I said, the two families never mixed socially. But I suppose Mrs Kodak must have dropped Lola off at Twenty-second Street occasionally, in the old days.

By this time I was blushing at the uncool idea that I

still looked like an eleven or twelve year old kid.

'Listen, we've already visited your house and spoken to your sister. She wasn't able to tell us anything new,' Lola's mother told me. 'But do you recall anything that might help the police find out where our daughter is?'

It was a desperate question when you thought about it. And I was struck by the fact that they'd called at my house. I told her that the only odd thing about the weekend had been on the Saturday after the basketball final; namely, one small package.

Dr Kodak stepped forward. 'You say she was upset when Tomas tried to hand her the packet?'

Hold it! It felt like the start of an inquisition; that cold grey eye, that hard-edged tone. There was something beaky and birdlike about his face; hooked nose, beady eye, and a plume of thick white hair rising from his forehead.

'Look, I've told you all I know, OK!' I put up both hands to get him to back off.

Dr Kodak turned to his wife. 'It's turning out exactly as I said. Somehow that brother of yours was behind this!'

Mrs Kodak met his gaze more coolly than I would've done in her shoes. It looked like a big family argument that had been going on for years. And no one was expressing any grief for the fact that Tomas was no longer with us.

'Fact; Tomas has been pushing Lola hard since she was thirteen years old. Fact; Lola asked us more than once for time off from full-time training. Fact; we relied on Tomas's opinion that even a short break would hold up her progress.' Dr Kodak hammered his forefinger into his other palm each time he said the word 'Fact'.

'Yes, and who was Lola trying to please when we advised her to stick with it?' Mrs Kodak pointed out. 'Not Tomas. Not me either.'

I got the picture; Lola trying her best to please Daddy, training hard, living up to his expectations. Whoa; that was *way* too much pressure.

'So, what's your idea?' I asked them. I'd told them all I knew. Now it was my turn to dig. 'Why would Lola run out on what could've been the biggest championship to date?'

Kodak looked at me with eyes of steel. 'She wouldn't,' he said simply. 'It's not in her nature to self-destruct in that way. She's too proud, she has too much self-respect. And she's not just some little hopeful up from the backwoods. Tennis is her life. The American Open is what she's been aiming at for six whole years!'

'It's a dog-eat-dog world' had been Dr Kodak's message. You win at all costs. Failure doesn't enter into it.

With his slight European accent stretching out his vowel sounds and clipping the ends off words, he scared me, I can tell you.

Kate too. We'd have liked a bit more worry over Lola, less of the Master-race stuff.

Anyway, we left the Kodaks to puzzle over the plastic envelope and got home as fast as we could, before anyone else gave us the third-degree.

'Line up the suspects,' Kate said before we split at the corner of Constitution Square. She counted them off on her fingers. 'There's Matthew King and a possible accomplice. There's Lendlova and a gang of illegal drugs suppliers.'

'And the Kodaks?' I cut in.

Kate wrinkled her nose. 'Kidnap their own daughter? Murder her own brother?'

'Listen, there's something with this whole family. Don't ask me!'

Reluctantly she added them to the list. 'How about jealous rivals on the circuit?' she suggested, holding up a fourth finger. Dog-eat-dog.

I said it was a possibility.

That gave us plenty to think about before we met up again at school next day.

I went home and heard on the TV news the unsurprising fact that police had made an arrest in the

Lola Kodak case. Matthew King's mugshot came up on screen. Detective Starkweather had been doing her stuff.

'You hear that?' Marcie yelled up to me from the basement. She was the only person home, as far as I could make out.

'Yeah. Wait!' I wanted to hear the rest.

They'd arrested King, then released him without charge. Now that was more interesting. The newsreader explained that the world's greatest tennis fan had been able to provide an alibi both for the time of Lola's so-called abduction and for Lendlova's killing. They didn't say what it was, but it must have been pretty watertight. Anyhow, they arrested him at Flushing Meadow during Bernice Matthieu's latest match. They questioned him then let him go.

'Great!' I flicked off the TV and went upstairs. I dumped my bag on the floor in the hall, took off my jacket, thinking, '*Lousy, god-awful day!*' Thinking, the only good thing about it had been the walk home with Kate.

Opened the door. Walked into my room. Saw Lola Kodak sitting on the bed.

7

Don't let me down, Joey! I thought. I looked round the class, saw his empty chair. How could I work out this Lola Kodak situation if Carter decided to crack up on me? We were a team; I needed him.

'What happened to Carter?' Zig said. Apparently, he had tickets for a big baseball game which he wanted to share.

'Why are you asking me?' I snapped back.

Zig backed off. 'Excuse me for opening my big mouth. I only know you walked home with him last night, that's all. But forget it. I'm sorry I breathed!'

'Yeah, sorry!' I murmured, genuine not sarcastic. What did Zig do, poor guy?

But Carter was never absent from school. He never got sick, he never bunked off. So how come his place was vacant on this morning of all mornings?

'Kate, Miss Slay wants to see you about tonight's tennis game.' Connie came in late with a message from the Sport teacher.

I excused myself from registration and slipped out.

But I didn't go looking for Slay, I went to Damien Carter's classroom instead.

I caught Joey's little brother coming out into the corridor and grabbed him. He's a younger version; the same short brown hair and the shy look from those eyes which are somewhere between grey and blue. I could tell at a glance that something bad had happened.

'Where's Carter?' I asked.

The kid ducked his head and made as if to march on. He swung round the corner and knocked me off-balance with the heavy bag which he carried. Another family trait; big bag slung over the shoulder. Swing it around, take no prisoners.

'Damien, hold it! You've gotta tell me; why isn't Joey in school?' The more he tried to avoid me in the crowded corridor, the more determined I was to get an answer.

'I don't know, OK! I can't tell you where he is. They said to keep my mouth shut.'

'Who's "they"? What happened?' I felt sick in my stomach as I dodged the bag again.

'Mom, Dad.' Damien came up against a bunch of kids standing in line outside the chemistry lab. He looked like he wished the ground would swallow him.

I felt sorry for him, and wildly worried now about Joey. So I backed off, said no problem, I'd catch up with his brother when he showed up. Underneath, my heart had begun to thump like it does when something real scary is going off.

No way was I going to go back to my classroom, pick up my bag and head for Math. Maybe I wasn't thinking clearly when I cut out through a side door in the Science block, across the schoolyard and out past the site superintendent's office. Officially I should have told someone what I planned to do, but that would have taken time and anyway they would've said no.

In any case, I was out on the sidewalk, picking up speed. Twenty-second Street was only a ten minute journey from school, but would there be a bus on the route I needed? I looked up and down the street, decided it would be quicker to walk, especially if I cut through the park.

Which is what I did. I ran under the Loop track, all the way across the park, up State Hill and over to Marytown, arriving at Carter's house at around 9.30 am.

Mrs Carter answered the door. She looked pale and drained, sighing when she saw me and asking me to step inside. When I say 'pale', I mean like she'd seen a ghost. The woman was traumatised, her hands were shaking, I could hardly hear what she said.

'What happened?' I gasped, out of breath from my

sprint across town. The house looked normal; newspapers and magazines scattered across the living-room carpet, the door to Marcie's basement studio standing open, Joey's giant schoolbag dumped at the bottom of the stairs.

'Kate, come into the kitchen, talk to the detectives!' Mrs Carter pleaded in this broken voice.

OK, so I'd seen the cop car by the kerb outside number 342 and, idiot me, hadn't paid it any attention. I was too busy catching my breath. Meanwhile, the bottom was dropping out of everyone's worlds. No Joey. Detectives at the house, for heaven's sake!

Mrs Carter was in a daze. Maybe they'd sedated her, or maybe it was the natural reaction to severe shock.

I recognised Detective Starkweather sitting at the kitchen table, but not the guy with her. He was short and bald, with what I took to be a permanently bad-tempered look about his mouth and heavy eyebrows. The eyebrows knitted together, like he'd taken too many lies and double-talk from petty criminals, drunks and crack addicts during his time on the Fortune City beat.

'Come in, Kate!' Starkweather's tone jarred, like this was a social visit. She wore beige and brown, she'd just visited her hairdresser and had some auburn highlights. 'This is Detective Sergeant Wade. I'm helping him look into this missing persons case.'

Did she say 'persons'? To my knowledge, there was only one, and that was Lola Kodak. I sat down warily at the table, across from Wade, who looked at me as if I was suspect number one.

'Kate, it's good that you showed up,' Starkweather confided. 'We think maybe you were the last to see Joey yesterday, and we're hoping you can fill in some of the gaps.'

Jeez, I could hardly breathe now. I felt the blood drain away from my face as I looked for clues on the faces of Wade, Starkweather and a silent Mrs Carter. Not to put too fine a point, I thought they were building up to telling me that Joey was dead.

'It's OK, it's not what you're thinking.' Detective Starkweather read my mind. 'I said missing persons, remember? The truth is that Joey and Marcie have vanished, and we're thinking that maybe, just maybe there's some connection with the Lola Kodak case.'

I got to speak with Mrs Carter alone after Starkweather and Wade had grilled me about Joey's last known movements after school the day before.

I told them that we'd walked home through the park and discussed Lola, that we'd come across Dr and Mrs Kodak by the monument. They questioned me pretty hard about that. Then I said that we'd left the park and split up on Constitution Square. Joey had planned to go right on home.

'He must have made it back this far,' Mrs Carter explained after the detectives had drunk up their coffee, told her to try not to worry, and left us in peace. 'His bag's in the hallway, his school jacket is hanging from the hook on his bedroom door.'

'And what about Marcie?' I was fitting together the pieces, not coming up with any sane reason why a brother and sister should vanish at the same time. I mean, one is worrying, but two missing family members is a million to one. Poor Mrs Carter.

'She stayed home yesterday to work in the studio.'

'By herself?'

Joey's mom nodded. 'The band has just finished recording a demo tape and Marcie was the one who was getting it ready to be sent off to one of the big record companies. Ocean and the other guys took day jobs to pay the studio hire fees. Ocean was real worried when I called him early this morning to tell him what happened.'

'So tell me!' I needed the details to bring the picture into focus. At the moment it was still blurred and crazy.

Mrs Carter told it like it was, her hands still trembling, her pale grey eyes wet with tears. 'Damien was the first to get back to an empty house. This was maybe a half after five. He didn't think anything; though if Joey does something different after school, he usually leaves a note. There was no note. Nothing. Then Joey's dad made it home from work half an hour later. He was cooking hamburgers when I got here at seven, saying why the heck couldn't Marcie and Joey let people know if they weren't going to show up for the evening meal.' The tears spilled over. She took a tissue from a half-empty box and dabbed her cheeks.

'Where's Mr Carter now?' I asked. Joey's dad didn't figure much at number 342. He got up, went to work at Hertz Rental Cars, came back, ate, went out again to play pool or poker. Nice guy, but not a major influence.

'He went to his job. He didn't want to call the cops in the first place, but by midnight I was going crazy.'

'So what did the cops say when you called?' I pictured the five or so hours of Mrs Carter growing more and more worried when neither Marcie nor Joey showed up.

'They said, give it until morning. In their opinion, it was unusual for *two* kids to run out on a place and for there to be anything seriously wrong. It seemed to them that they would eventually show up of their own accord.'

'Yeah.' This had occurred to me too. But then again, no. Not at this point in time, with the Lola Kodak thing going on. And with Marcie being Lola's friend, and Lola staying at their house, and Tomas Lendlova being shot in the yard out back. 'So when did the cops finally decide to pay you a visit?'

'I called them again at around seven thirty this morning. I got Detective Starkweather and she was the one who decided it was worth putting in some police time. She brought Sergeant Wade with her and we've been through the whole thing: how Joey did come back after school, how Marcie was working in the basement up to a certain point, because I called home and spoke to her around four.'

'But both Joey and Marcie had left the house by the time Damien got home at five thirty?' I checked.

Mrs Carter nodded and sighed. 'I've been through this so many times!'

'And there was nothing; no clues, no sign of a struggle?'

This time she shook her head. 'The cops found just one little thing: a Greyhound bus ticket on Joey's bed.'

'Where from?'

'From a little town east of here called Ashwood. One way ticket; Ashwood to Fortune City. Which is a mystery, since so far as I know Joey never went near the place.'

I stored this fact and stood up from the table. There

was no point re-doing the detective thing of telling Mrs Carter not to worry, but I did anyway. 'Listen,' I said, 'I'm sure we'll find Joey and Marcie soon, and everything will be back to normal.'

You say these things without meaning them, and the person you say them to nods and sighs and doesn't believe a word you say. We go through the rituals. Inside, we're each at screaming pitch.

I went straight from Twenty-second Street to Heaven's Gate. This was a time to use my connections with Angelworks and the mega-powerful media personage of Angel Christian.

'Why aren't you in school?' Dad demanded. He was busy with the schedule for filming the following Tuesday's documentary, planning to get Angel and the crew in the right places at the right times.

Angel herself was with her futurologist in some private part of the sprawling house. She surrounds herself with these people: a woman who works on auras, a feng-shui consultant, someone who tells her which colours to wear.

I told Dad what had happened at the Carters' house. 'It's crazy. It doesn't make any sense. But I know it's something really bad!'

He looked at me and made a snap judgement that

brought him down in the same place I was standing. He knew Joey wasn't the kind to float off for no reason. 'OK, what do you want to do about it?'

'We have to find out what happened!' I was practically yelling, until he put his arm around my shoulder and led me to a seat at his desk. 'It's connected with Lola!' I tried to explain my gut feeling, to convince him that this whole mess linked up somehow.

'Sit. Breathe deep. Count to ten.'

I breathed, then nodded. 'Dad, you and Angel are still working on this big tennis circuit deal, aren't you?'

I knew that next week's documentary was a follow-up to 'What Makes Lola Tick?' and that Angel was hoping to dig the dirt on some of the other major women players. I didn't know what she'd found, but I was thinking that maybe it would shed some light.

'We've been investigating a couple of big names,' Dad agreed. 'Angel's good. She makes connections, asks the right questions. I think we might be on to something important.'

While he explained where they were at, I glanced at the bank of monitors above the desk. There was footage of Bernice Matthieu, and a screen that showed the action live from Flushing Meadow.

'What exactly have you got so far?' I asked.

(*Joey, where are you? Joey, don't do this to me!*)

Dad tapped a few keys and brought up an image on the nearest screen. It was Matthew King with his neat little goatee beard and unreliable, easy-over fried-egg eyes.

'King was arrested eighteen months ago for stalking Bernice Matthieu. It didn't make the headlines because Matthieu felt it would encourage copycat crimes, so the cops played it down. In the end, King got six months suspended sentence. Angel had a couple of researchers go through the court records, and found out that the judge ordered psychiatric reports before she passed sentence.'

I took this in, getting the feeling that there was more to the Matthew King story that kept him right in the middle of the picture as far as Lola Kodak was concerned. But I was disappointed in what Dad had to add.

'Six months later, King was still travelling the tennis circuit, drooling over Bernice, and it was clear that the suspended sentence hadn't acted in any way to put him off. This is where Bernice's husband, Alain, stepped in.'

This was the first I'd heard of a husband for the Women's number two. I guess I looked surprised.

Dad smiled. 'Tennis players have private lives just like the rest of us, remember. Only, most choose not to splash it across the media. Anyhow, the word is, Alain Matthieu eventually had it up to here with King. They ended up having a fight outside a night club in London. King was stabbed in the stomach and had to be stitched up as a matter of urgency. Nothing was proved. No charges were brought. But Angel says her source of information is reliable.'

'So what kind of guy is Matthieu?'

Dad flicked up another still picture on to the screen. I saw a very good-looking face; fair hair, clean-cut, movie-star handsome.

'That's him. But don't be deceived by the looks. Alain Matthieu should come with a health warning.'

I turned to Dad. 'How come?'

'Angel's researchers again. They dug the dirt on Monsieur Matthieu. The guy has a history. A couple of convictions for violent assaults, a possible link with a drugs scandal in the Men's game in the late eighties.'

'OK. What else?' Time was ticking by. I didn't feel much closer to picking up a clue about Lola, Joey or Marcie.

Dad turned to a different screen to point out a shot of Lola's parents, Dr and Mrs Kodak, sitting courtside at one of their daughter's big wins. They smiled and applauded and looked proud as she lifted the trophy. 'Shock, horror number two!' he told me. 'Angel's discovered that the Internal Revenue Service are expressing an interest in exactly what happened to two million dollars worth of Lola's prize money which she won before the age of sixteen.'

'Two million!' I echoed. For that kind of money I might even let Slay bully me into improving my game!

'Before she was sixteen, remember. So the money went into a trust fund run by Dr and Mrs Kodak. And now it turns out that quite a lot of it was never declared to the taxman. Tut-tut. And it gets worse; the parents face a stiff fine and even gaol if it can be proved that they deliberately cheated and intended to defraud the government.'

'But no one knows about this?' I studied the two smiling faces, thought that no wonder the parents had been so keen for Lola to play the circuit as much as possible. They were stashing some of the prize money themselves.

'Not yet. The investigation is still underway.' Dad swivelled his chair away from the monitors towards me, and spun me round to face him in turn. 'One last thing,' he said.

'Yeah?'

(*Joey, I'm doing my best here. I'm trying to get a hold of a lead that will help!*)

'Angel came up with an interesting new fact about

the night Lola disappeared.'

'Really!'

(*This could be it! Please, God, let it be the one!*)

Dad landed it right in my lap.

'Lola was seen right after she split from Lendlova. He'd stopped for gas, remember? And she went to the rest-room?'

I nodded. 'Go on!'

'Well, someone saw her climb on to a bus on the highway shortly afterwards. At least, it was a girl matching Lola's description. She was alone. She bought a ticket from the driver and headed for Fortune City.'

'Where was this?' I begged. Which is when it finally clicked into place.

'A small town east of here which no one ever heard of. Almost too small to figure on the map. A place by the name of Ashwood.'

8

I read a demolition site notice as they drove us in here. 'Unsafe Building. Keep out!' I wasn't meant to see it, but there was a moment when my blindfold came loose, before they jerked my head away from the car window and re-tied the knot.

Then they bundled us out of the car, completely blind, and kicked us down some steps. A metal door scraped shut behind us. When I say 'us', I mean me, Marcie and Lola, all trussed up like Thanksgiving turkeys. When I say 'they', I don't have the faintest idea who I'm talking about.

Flashback. Action Replay.

'You hear that?' Marcie yelled from the basement. She'd been working all day on a demo tape, but was taking a break to listen to the TV news.

'Yeah. Wait!' It was me cutting in, wanting to hear the full bulletin about Matthew King.

(*Dying quote from Lendlova: 'She made a run for it, but they took her anyway.'*

Me: 'Man, who are we talking about?'
Lendlova: 'Matthew. Game, set and match!')

I heard that the cops arrested him then let him go. Something about an alibi. So what had Lendlova been talking about when he named the mad fan as the guy who beat him in the end?

'Great!' I tramped upstairs, not in the best mood of my entire life. I went into my room and found Lola Kodak sitting there.

'Cool it, Joey!' Marcie told me. She'd followed me up, acted like it was nothing that the missing golden girl of tennis had turned up on my bed. 'Quit making like a goldfish, and go fetch us all a can of Coke from the ice-box.'

'No way. Not until you tell me what's happening!' I slammed the door shut and kept my eyes on Lola. This was hard to believe.

'She needed a place to lie low, and she was totally desperate, so she came here,' Marcie explained calmly. She was still in her 'Love and Peace' gear: long cotton skirt, Indian sandals, silver beads in her hair. 'I said we'd help hide her.'

'Hide from who?' My voice came out strangled. What was this suddenly; a refugee camp for displaced sportspeople?

Lola sat cross-legged, her red hair loose over her

shoulders, a purse containing money and make-up scattered over my pillow.

'From the guys who tried to kidnap her outside the gas station in Ashwood,' Marcie told me with all the patience she could muster. Which was rapidly running out, by the way. '*You* tell him, Lola,' she muttered, going off to fetch the ice-cold Cokes herself.

'Wait, wait!' I held up my hands, backed off to the window overlooking the yard. The window was open because of the heat, a newly washed towel and a pair of my shorts hanging on the fire-escape to dry. 'Let me get this straight. You're here looking for shelter until you handle some kind of crisis. And this crisis involves some guys who tried to snatch you. So tell me, did you run away from Lendlova, or were you kidnapped?'

'Both.' Lola's relaxed position on the bed was assumed, I realised. In fact, the way she twisted her fingers together showed she was uptight. 'I decided to make a run for it on Sunday night, after Uncle Tomas came here to pick me up and drive me over to the airport to catch our plane to Flushing Meadow.'

I leaned against the window frame and nodded, glad of a breath of cool air from the shady yard. Did Lola know what had happened to the late, lamented Uncle Tomas since she last saw him, I wondered.

'The weird thing is, I caught a glimpse of a black car

following us, but I pushed it out of my mind. I guess I was too busy planning my escape.'

'Why run away from Lendlova?' My natural curiosity overcame my surprise at last. I mean, I had a hundred questions I wanted to ask.

'You know the answer,' Lola said quietly, uncrossing her legs, standing up and throwing small items back into her purse. 'You saw him hand me that envelope, didn't you?'

I was by now fully paying attention. 'Sure. But I didn't know you'd seen me there in the doorway.'

She shrugged. 'If you thought it was drugs in that packet, you were right.'

Ten out of ten for deduction. Grade A student. Maybe I'd be a cop when I left college. Then again, I might have to work alongside Starkweather. 'Tomas wanted you to take them to improve your performance at the American Open?' I prompted.

'He said it's what everyone else was doing. The drugs were new and none of the dope tests could detect them. They'd give me more stamina, more strength. Without them, I'd be bound to lose to Matthieu in the first round.' Slowly, deliberately, Lola gave me the low-down on Lendlova. 'I said no; no way. I'd rather play fair and lose, if that was how it turned out.'

'Had it happened before?'

'A couple of times. Earlier this year at Wimbledon, for instance. I said no then too, and got through to the quarter-finals on my own merits.' Lola zipped up her purse, then turned to take a can of drink from Marcie as she came back into the room. 'But Uncle Tomas kept up with the pressure. One time, about a couple of weeks back, I told him enough! I even threatened to go to the international authorities and cause a scandal; tell them how many players were involved in taking these new drugs. Tomas said I wouldn't dare. If I did, my life would be in danger. That was pretty scary, I can tell you.'

'So you didn't name names?' Well, I could easily understand that. It would take a lot of guts to expose something like this. And you wouldn't be number one in the popularity stakes amongst your fellow players. Particularly the guilty ones.

Lola sighed.

I recalled how tired and upset she'd looked last Saturday by the lockers in school. She'd been through a lot, and I still wasn't fully up to date. 'OK, so you refused to take the drugs, but he was still putting on pressure and you were threatening to blow the whole thing sky-high. So you thought your only way out was to run. You get as far as the gas station and you seize your chance. Then what?'

'Remember I mentioned a black car following us? Well,

I headed for the rest-room while Tomas filled up with gas, but instead I cut down the side of the building, across a forecourt in front of a small diner by the highway. I ducked behind a row of trucks parked there, planning to hide, lose Tomas, then wait for the next bus back to Fortune City. Only, I never made it across the parking-lot.'

'The black car was full of guys who are basically drugs suppliers to the world of professional sport.' Marcie sounded like she thought we needed to move on. Obviously she'd heard it once already. 'They'd picked up from Tomas that Lola was very unhappy about their "product". Like, no way was she going to wear their logo on her tennis shirt!'

'I'd become a threat,' Lola added. 'So they put someone on my tail and watched every move. When I made the break from Tomas, that was when they decided it was time to act.'

'Very subtle,' I sneered. 'Like, seizing a famous tennis player in the parking-lot of a two-bit diner isn't going to draw the attention of the world press!'

Lola forced a smile. 'What do those guys care? By the time anyone had worked out what happened, I'd be off the scene permanently. No evidence. And they'd deny everything. End of problem. Only they weren't so efficient as they planned.'

'They lost her between a Dodge Utility Vehicle and a

Mack truck,' Marcie said, proud of Lola's ability to give professional hitmen the slip.

'The black car drove full-speed out of a side alley, across the forecourt, in full view of Uncle Tomas and the clerk at the till in the gas station.' Lola completed the picture. 'I saw the unsuspecting driver of the Dodge come out of the diner, get in his cab and start the engine. I had the cover of the big truck between me and the car. So I vaulted up into the back of the Dodge and lay down flat amongst a collection of empty plastic canisters. Not a soul knew what had happened, not even the Dodge driver. It was like I'd vanished into thin air and left the guys in the black car as well as Uncle Tomas standing.'

'Neat.' Lola was going up and up in my estimation. I pictured the scene between the guys in the black car and Uncle Tomas as she exited in the Dodge. They'd be too busy arguing and passing the buck to notice her reach the highway, jump out of the slow-moving truck and hop on to the next convenient Greyhound bus.

Well, that was the highpoint; me, Marcie and Lola enjoying the victory over organised crime, sipping cold Coke in my room late Wednesday afternoon.

Lola was telling us that at least three of the top ten names in the Women's game were known on the inside to be regularly taking these new performance enhancers.

'Who?' Marcie asked, eager to be in on the secret.

'You don't want to know,' Lola warned. And she said she cared too much about Marcie ever to name names. 'Information like that is dangerous. If they know you know, you never walk down the street in safety again.'

Laid back, innocent Marcie said Lola was over-reacting.

Lola said, 'No way. Believe me.'

Then three guys blasted up the fire escape, through the window.

Thirty seconds and it was over.

One went for Lola with a blindfold and a gag, ready with the rope to tie her hands behind her back. The second got Marcie, who yelled and screamed until the guy got out a gun and pointed it at her. She went silent then.

Me too. I'd got in one punch and a kick at my well-built guy before, out of the corner of my eye I saw the barrel two inches from my sister's head. The distraction allowed Mr Muscles to move in with a gun of his own.

If we wanted to live we had to go quietly down the fire escape with our hands tied – as far as the black car with shaded windows parked in the yard.

There was no one around as we exited in single file. Footsteps on the metal staircase, a couple of minutes more and the car doors had slammed shut on us, the engine was racing and we came roaring out of the alley on to Twenty-second Street.

You measure the seconds and minutes when you think

there's a good chance they could be your last.

That was yesterday.

They blindfolded Marcie and me to match Lola as they drove us across Marytown, so that by the time we reached our destination – this demolition site I mentioned earlier – we had no way of knowing how long we'd driven or where we were.

It's what they do to hostages. They disorientate you and refuse to speak to you. They keep you in the dark and make you think that any minute, any second, they could come back into the room and put a bullet through your head.

9

Ashwood! Lola had been seen boarding a bus in this no-mark, two-bit town. And there was the bus ticket which the cops had found on Joey's bed.

It didn't take a genius to put these two things together and come out with the answer that Lola Kodak had been back to number 342.

'Hold it!' Dad blocked my way as I made a sudden dash to the door. 'Why do I get the feeling that you plan to do something rash?'

'Dad, please; I gotta go! Carter's dug himself in deep. He needs help!'

(*Joey, I'm on my way! Wherever you are, don't do anything stupid. I mean it, I'm bringing help!*)

Dad stood firm, arms folded across his chest. 'Am I missing something here? Explain to this slow old brain of mine just what is the connection between what I just said about Lola getting on to a bus and Joey being in trouble?'

'Ashwood!' I cried. 'Bus ticket . . . bed!' I was pretty garbled, but I managed to make Dad understand. 'Say

Lola was on the run from someone other than Tomas Lendlova . . .' It was the line of thought that Carter and I had developed yesterday afternoon. Which felt like centuries ago now.

(*Joey, hang on! I'm working it out as fast as I can!*)

'Hold it one more time!' Dad grabbed me by the arms and made me sit at his desk. 'Like, who? Who besides Lendlova would be looking for Lola?'

I shook my head until my brain hurt. 'That I can't say. But, suppose there's some huge drugs scandal we don't know about. Say Lendlova was only a small player when he tried to force those performance enhancers on to Lola. And there's a big, international organisation out there. They'd be pretty keen for Lola to keep quiet . . .'

This all made sense to me, even if the look on Dad's face told me he wasn't convinced.

'So when she gave Uncle Tomas the slip, they'd be on her tail, wouldn't they? She'd be so scared she wouldn't know what to do. So where could she find a safe place to hide? Somewhere out of the tennis world completely. Not her parents' place in Pennsylvania; that would be too obvious. Where?' I waited for Dad to make the connection.

'The Carters' house?'

'Yeah! Lola makes her way back to Twenty-second

Street in secret, hoping to lose whoever's following her. She waits until there's only Marcie in the house, then she goes in and begs her old school friend for help. Marcie would say, "Yeah, cool," without thinking twice. She'd suspect that maybe Lola was paranoid and that the whole drugs mess was a figment of her imagination.' Marcie was like that; partly on a different planet. No sense of reality.

Dad was getting it at last. He was slowly nodding and backing off from my chair, giving me the space to stand up and pace the floor.

'So Marcie gives Lola Joey's room again. And Carter turns up after school yesterday to find his bed occupied by an unexpected guest. He's just getting used to the idea of hiding a famous fugitive for a second time, when the drugs guys break up the cosy scene.'

Dad took a deep breath and blew out through his cheeks. 'You're saying they broke in and took all three of them hostage without so much as a struggle?'

I was by the open door, and this time he wasn't blocking my way.

'What do you plan to do; call the cops?'

'*You* could do that, Dad. Tell them about the fact that Lola was seen boarding the bus in Ashwood.'

'OK. But how about you?'

'I'm gonna make my way to Joey's place eventually

to speak with Mrs Carter. But first I need to know where the Kodaks are staying.' This was where Angel's computer files might come in useful. I thought maybe her researchers would have a hotel name on record. I dashed across the room, pressed keys and brought up the names, Dr and Mrs Kodak, the Pennsylvania address, the place they'd checked into in Fortune City. I memorised this; Monument Hotel, State Hill.

'OK, you bring them up-to-date,' Dad agreed. 'And let's meet up with the cops at Carter's place.'

Deal. I was out of there, leaving my dad busy on the phone, without telling him the real reason I wanted to talk with the Kodaks.

Now, this was it. I had a clear memory of Joey's and my unexpected meeting with Lola's parents by the monument in the park. They'd stepped out from under the flags and given Joey the third degree. And they'd told us that they'd already grilled Marcie.

So get this; Herr Doktor and Mrs Kodak must have interviewed Carter's sister and all the time their precious daughter, Lola, had been holed up in Joey's bedroom!

Well, I needed to speak to them about this.

Monument Hotel was the big white building at the

top of State Hill, overlooking the park. The best hotel in town, it had wide steps flanked at the top by tall white pillars, and one of those old revolving doors made of polished wood and shiny, bevelled glass.

The doorman in the grey uniform with gold braid trim gave me a look when I ran up the steps two at a time. But, hey this is a free country and all men are born equal . . .

I was across the acres of red carpet, ringing the bell in reception before the doorman had decided I was weird but harmless. 'Dr and Mrs Kodak!' I gasped at the young guy. White shirt, dark, wavy hair, and a name badge: Kevin.

'Who shall I say?' Kevin said politely. Never mind that I was a breathless, windswept kid with apparently no manners.

'Tell them it's Kate Brennan. It's concerning their daughter!'

This brought them down in the elevator within a minute, I can tell you.

Mrs Kodak met me first, half-running across the lobby, grasping both my hands. 'Did you get some news?' she begged.

She was a different woman from the one I'd met just twenty-four hours earlier. The dark suit and white blouse were gone. Now she wore loose trousers and a

T-shirt, no make-up, and she looked like she hadn't slept much.

I told her that the cops had a new lead, that was all. How could you trust a woman who had cheated her own daughter out of a couple of million? I mean, she might look sorry about things now, but people like the Kodaks aren't like the rest of us. So how long would it be before she started mislaying the cheques again?

'I came to ask you a couple of questions,' I went on.

Dr Kodak was holding it together better than his wife. He hadn't deserted the grey suit and dark blue tie. His face still gave that hawkish impression. 'Make it fast,' he snapped, looking at his watch. 'If the police have something new, I need to call them. Wait for them to contact us and we'd still be here tomorrow.'

See what I mean? Sniping at the cops, instead of worrying about his daughter.

'You say you called at Twenty-second Street yesterday afternoon?' I reminded him.

'What of it?'

Defences up as high as the walls of Fort Knox. Eyes glittering with a steely glint. Like he's warning me not to try and trip him up.

'I need to know, did you notice anything going on in the street?'

Something clicked. He gave a small nod. 'OK, I get

it. This has to do with the Carter kids' disappearance, not with Lola.'

Deep breath. 'Maybe both,' I told him. But I wasn't going to spell it out. Like I said, how could you possibly trust these guys? 'Please, Dr Kodak, could you try to remember if you saw anything unusual outside number 342.'

He shrugged and walked off without a word, reached over the reception desk and took a hold of Kevin's phone without even asking. He dialled a number and said, 'Get me Detective Sergant Wade.'

'Mrs Kodak?' I turned to the wife.

'I don't remember anything,' she whispered, covering her tired face with a hand that sported two giant diamonds. 'These last four days have been a nightmare. It's all so muddled . . . !'

'Like some guy hanging around in the street, watching the Carters' house?' I kept at her, knowing this was important. The Kodaks' visit had probably coincided with the stake-out of number 342 by the people who were now holding Joey, Marcie and Lola prisoner. I hoped. Anything else just didn't bear thinking about. 'Like a car parked by the sidewalk?' I suggested.

The hand fell from her face and she looked at me with sudden focus. I could see Lola there; the concentration when the eyes narrow and home in on an object. 'There *was* a car,' she told me, obviously reliving the moment. 'It was parked opposite. There were two men leaning against it.'

'What colour was the car?' I pounced on this.

'Black.'

'And just two men?'

'Three. There was a third guy in the car, but I couldn't see him clearly because the windshield was shaded.' The details were coming back to her. 'I noticed them particularly because they were – well, they didn't fit in with the area. The car was an executive model, the men wore good, lightweight suits.'

I nodded like crazy. Dr Kodak was finishing his call to the cops, barking some orders down the phone. 'You didn't recognise them by any chance?'

Mrs Kodak shook her head. 'Tall guys, wearing shades, definitely interested in us going up the steps to number 342.' She paused and sighed. 'My mind wasn't on them at the time. There was one other odd thing, though.'

God, was I nodding, praying and hoping.

'The third one; the one inside the car. I remember thinking, "I know you!" – then I dismissed it.'

'Who did you think it was?' I was pressing hard, wanting an answer before Dr Hawkeye rejoined us. He had a way of dampening all conversation.

His wife saw him coming. She laughed unconvincingly and waved away her remark as she spoke. 'This is just silly, but I did think for a split second that the driver of the car was Alain Matthieu.'

Wade had told Dr Kodak to head straight over to Twenty-second Street. I wasn't too proud to beg a ride in their taxi, knowing that was where the action was going to be.

I was right; the place was crawling.

Mrs Carter looked like it had gone way beyond her and Mr Carter was having to hold the fort. I was impressed; he let me and Dr and Mrs Kodak through the door, but told the press crew gathered outside to get lost in no uncertain terms.

The journalists, like bees round a honey-pot, had picked up the fact that there was new activity at number 342.

'Jackals,' Joey's dad said as he closed the door behind us. 'Cops, your dad and Angel Christian all in the kitchen,' he informed me, taking charge of Mrs Kodak and leading her upstairs to Joey's room to show her Lola's last known whereabouts. He was considerate and kind; after all, they were both in the same boat now.

In the kitchen there was a lot of noise and confusion.

For some reason, Mr Carter didn't count Angel as part of the press gang, so she was there with my dad and a cameraman, conducting interviews, building up footage for next Tuesday's show. At the time of my arrival, she was quizzing Wade about the bus ticket, asking him to guess how long Lola could have been holed up at number 342. However, when Dr Kodak came in behind me, he put a stop to the filming and accused the police of wasting precious time.

Me and Starkweather made an opportune exit at that point.

'Nice work, Kate.' The detective congratulated me at the foot of the stairs, waiting for Mr Carter to escort Mrs Kodak down to join the argument in the kitchen. 'The Ashwood link gives us a nice lead.'

I had to pause until the kitchen door was closed again and the noise died down. 'Thanks. But we gotta move fast. Now that we know Joey and Marcie's disappearance is definitely linked with Lola's, we can't waste any time.' I could lose Carter here if we weren't careful. In fact, I could've lost him already. My stomach turned and dived.

(*Joey, for God's sake, where are you?*)

'Come upstairs.' Starkweather took me by the arm and led me into Joey's room. She sat me on the bed, all motherly. 'OK?' she asked.

I couldn't speak, but I nodded. If I spoke, I would've cried for sure.

'Look, I know you're worried about Joey. We all are. But we're working on it, OK?'

One more nod.

'And you know him better than most; you can help.'

'How?' I let myself slump, head down. It was like my head had been hit hard. It was spinning, I was dizzy, I couldn't take much more.

('I did think for a split second that the driver of the car was Alain Matthieu.' . . . *OK, Joey, I need you to help me figure that one out. It blows my mind. I mean, exactly how come Matthieu's name crops up here?*)

'For instance,' Starkweather said, 'how does Joey react in a crisis? Is he likely to panic or keep his cool?'

'He won't freak out,' I told her. 'He'll keep his head, think his way through it.'

'Well, that's good. If we know he won't do anything crazy, that gives him a higher chance of survival in a situation like this.'

'I'm not saying he won't try to make a run for it if he gets the chance,' I warned.

'But he won't provoke violence, that's the point.' Starkweather walked to the open window and looked out over the fire escape. 'There were no signs of a struggle,' she reminded herself. 'So there was no actual fight.'

Personally I didn't find this surprising. Or reassuring. What it meant was that the guys who'd taken Joey and co. had guns. You don't argue with a gun.

The detective looked over her shoulder at me. 'Joey means a lot to you, doesn't he, Kate?'

It was another of those occasions when I couldn't speak. I just got up from the bed and wandered to the window, looked down on the yard where Lendlova had been shot.

'Did you rule Matthew King out of the killing for good?' I asked, changing the subject. There was tape marking the spot where he had fallen, a bird's eye view of the murder scene.

'Yep.' Starkweather remained thoughtful, staring down. 'The guy's a weirdo, but not a homicidal one. And he has witnesses to say he was watching Bernice Matthieu play a mixed doubles match on court number two at Flushing Meadow when Lendlova was shot.'

'Then why did Lendlova name him?' I wanted to know. It was the thing that snarled up my brain most of all. A dying man, his killer's name on his lips.

('Matthew. Game, set and match.'

Come on, Kate; you're smart. Work it out.

'*Matthew*.' Matthew King.

109

'*Matthew*.' With Lendlova's choking, gasping last breath.

I leaned over him, heard him whisper the name with that faint Czechoslovakian accent.

'*Matthew . . . Matthe . . . Matthieu!*')

10

It's dark. Your mouth is taped, you're blindfolded, your hands are tied.

With the three senses you have left, you work out that the place you're in is damp, cold and probably underground because the traffic sounds a long way off and overhead.

You listen a lot, because the next sound could be footsteps. And then you have a decision to make: 'Do I yell out for help on the chance that it's an innocent passer-by? Or do I say my prayers because these are the guys who tore me out of my life, threatened and terrified me, tied me up and dumped me here in the first place?'

I tell you, this was the most helpless I'd felt in my whole life.

At first, Lola and Marcie had cried. They took it in turns. Marcie stopping made Lola begin.

I fumbled my way round what I took to be a basement, stumbling into each of them in turn. I made some sounds through my gag which were meant to communicate a 'Don't panic' message. It was kind of our kidnappers not to tie our feet, I thought. At least we could walk around and blunder into each other.

After a while, Marcie and Lola sat down on the floor, huddled side by side for comfort, I guess.

I went on stumbling and blundering, working out that this basement was completely empty. It was square, twenty paces by twenty paces, with twelve steps up to a rusty metal door. There was no fresh air vent of any kind, and definitely no window.

Once I'd done this exploration maybe twenty times, I had to accept there was no way out.

But there were improvement to be made. We didn't have to live with this tape over our mouths for a start. OK, so I'm no contortionist, and my own hands were tied behind my back, making access to my mouth impossible. But if I sidled up to Marcie, making like a chimpanzee – 'Uh-uh . . . uh-uh-uh!' – and got into position so that my mouth was up against her hands, which were also tied behind her back, I was pretty sure she'd soon get the idea.

'Uh-uh-uh!' she said back, when I knelt beside her.

I shoved my face against her fingers and waited for her to unpeel the tape. 'Ouch!'

Being able to breathe through my mouth again was a great relief. I turned my back to her and spoke my first words since we were taken prisoner. 'Take off my blindfold!'

She fumbled and did this.

'Now untie me!'

'Uh-uh!' Marcie argued back.

'What? Oh, OK!' I guessed she wanted me to remove her gag and blindfold first. And Lola's. I did it as fast as I could, even though it made more sense to me for her to work on my hands first to give me more freedom of movement to take away their tapes and gags. It took some time for my eyes to get used to the pitch-black space, but by the time I came back to Marcie for her to untie my hands, I could make out the pale blob of her face and a very faint glint of silver from the beads in her hair.

I guess this pantomime took thirty minutes or more, but by that time I had no idea how long we'd been locked up; hours definitely, possibly overnight and today was already Thursday.

'Thank God we're free!' Marcie gasped, rubbing her wrists where the rope had dug in.

'Free' is relative, not absolute. It didn't need me to point out that we were still trapped in a black hole in the ground and that for all we knew the three guys responsible had gone away from here and thrown away the key.

But there was no doubt some relief to be had in being able to talk again. Even if it was to admit how dead-scared we all were.

'We could starve!' Marcie whispered. 'And no one would know until it was too late!'

They were demolishing the building that stood above this living-grave of ours. I pictured the bulldozers moving in, swinging those giant iron balls suspended from chains, sending them crashing into the walls. The bricks would crumble and crash down on top of the entrance to the basement. We'd be sealed in. Period.

'They wouldn't do that!' Lola cried in a thin, horrified voice.

Who was she kidding? I went up the steps and kicked the door, came back down, saw by the illuminated dial on my watch that it was Thursday, half after two in the afternoon, going on for twenty-four hours since we'd been snatched.

11

Matthieu, not Matthew! Alain Matthieu, not Matthew King!

It was Lendlova's accent that had thrown Joey and me, that had snarled us up and stopped us thinking clearly to correctly identify the man in that upper storey window, who pointed his telescopic sights with fatal accuracy down into the yard behind Joey's house.

'Pull out everything we know on Bernice Matthieu's husband!' Starkweather radioed headquarters after I'd managed to explain our mistake. She'd gone downstairs to the kitchen to inform Sergeant Wade and say she thought I was on to something hot.

(*Sorry it took me so long, Joey! Please God we're not too late!*)

Angel and Dad were on the ball too, reaching for their laptop and tapping in Matthieu's name. They had all the relevant stuff on file for their documentary.

'December '88, Alain Matthieu was found guilty in a French court of supplying steroids to two of the top men tennis players.' Angel read from the small screen in front of her. 'He served six months. This was before he married Bernice, which was in 1993.'

'And then there was an incident in London eighteen months back,' Dad reminded her. 'The rumour was that Alain Matthieu had stabbed Bernice's stalker in a fight outside a club, but the case never came to court. And the whole thing was pretty much hushed up.'

'But if it's true, it shows that Matthieu can turn to violence,' Angel insisted. 'He likes to present a cool playboy front, but there's a darker side too.'

I glanced at Dr and Mrs Kodak and the Carters as Angel said this, to see how they were taking it. The doctor was reading the screen over Angel's shoulder, while his wife stood isolated by the door. Mr and Mrs Carter stood together, holding hands.

'I'm more interested in the drugs conviction,' Wade said, bullet-headed, with no noticeable neck to speak of. He came at the problem like a bull, head down, charging. 'I'm making a connection with the fact that Lendlova was seen by Joey pushing a packet of what we take to be illegal substances on to Lola Kodak the day before she disappeared. I'm looking at a history of organised crime, involving both Lendlova and Matthieu . . . and spare me the Hollywood image, puh-lease!'

* * *

On the living-room TV, which we could hear through open doors, we learned that coverage of Flushing Meadow had reached the third round of the Women's Singles tournament.

'Bernice Matthieu is powering her way through this match!' the commentator said between games. She was winning three games to love in the second set, first set to Matthieu.

'Yes,' his fellow-presenter agreed. 'Bernice obviously has her sights set on reaching the final and taking the US Championship trophy for the first time in her career.'

'Which would raise her ranking to number one in the world . . .'

'Phenomenal achievement . . . remarkable improvement in every aspect of her game.'

'You notice there's no loving husband in the family and friends box,' Starkweather remarked after she went to take a look at the match and came back into the kitchen.

Wade grunted. 'What do we know about Alain, apart from his criminal record? Who are his associates? What are his business interests?'

The questions seemed pretty general to me, and not

leading where we needed to go, which was to pin down what Mattthieu might have been doing outside number 342 yesterday afternoon, and where he'd taken Marcie, Joey and Lola. I'd reached the point where I wanted to leave this hot, crowded little room, go outside and get some air.

But Angel and her laptop stopped me in my tracks. 'I have something here,' she volunteered, managing to sound both modest yet sure of herself in the same breath. She was sitting upright in her cool, pale blue shift dress, manicured hands poised over the tiny computer. 'Matthieu's known to run several manufacturing companies, all connected with sport in some way. He makes golfing equipment in New Mexico, co-owns a high-energy glucose drink factory in Florida. And see this; he runs an outfit called Pro-Sport, which produces mass-market sports clothing.'

'Based where?' Starkweather squinted down at the screen.

'There are small factories in California and New Jersey,' Angel said. 'But the main production unit and the head office is . . . guess where?'

The detective read out the answer. 'Fairview Industrial Estate.'

'Which is ten miles out of Fortune City,' Wade concluded, directing his broad shoulders towards the door and squeezing his bulky frame between Mrs Kodak and Joey's parents. 'C'mon, Starkweather, we're out of here!'

12

If I'd committed a major homicide in a state where they still have the electric chair, I'd fight for a reprieve until the very last second, believe me.

I mean, being told when you're gonna die, so that all element of surprise is taken out of it, has got to be the worst.

I know what I'm saying here, because 'condemned' is the word I'd use to describe how it felt to Lola, me and Marcie down in that black, locked basement.

When I wasn't kicking doors and busy going crazy, I was thinking of Kate.

Sometimes it would be: *OK, Kate, I'm believing in telepathy all of a sudden. I'm willing you to pick up the signals. Three guys came in through the fire escape and jumped us, OK? We need you to find us pretty damn fast. The only problem, even if this thought-reading stuff works, is that I can't tell you who they are or where they brought us!*

Then I would give up on that and just picture her. I could see her on the tennis court at school, while me and

Zig and the rest of the guys tried out for the basketball team. Kate looks cool even when she's hot. Her face doesn't turn red and blotchy. She has a way of holding a tennis racket and hitting the ball that you would call graceful.

Or I could see her close-up, giving me a look that says, '*Yeah, Carter; so when are you gonna ask me out on an official date? Never, that's when!*' She's half-smiling and turning away because this is a joke we've had going for some time. Like, 'Never' is when I'm gonna admit that we're an item.

We both prefer it that way.

Only, now I wish I'd addressed the issue; said, 'Kate, I'm never gonna meet another girl like you in a million years.'

Being entombed turns you sentimental. In real life, I'd never commit myself that far.

'So, tell me before I die. Who did this to us?' Marcie broke her silence at around 3.00pm.

We'd listened to a heavy truck trundle to a halt not too far from where we were imprisoned, opted for keeping quiet until we were sure it wasn't our three guys in the lightweight suits and sunshades. Mind you, heavy truck wasn't their style. Smooth limo, purring engine, ignoring speed limits was more their thing.

'Don't say we're gonna die!' Lola shuddered. The cold had got to her, and the dark limbo.

'C'mon, tell us everything!' Marcie implied that it was the least she could do. 'Begin with your Uncle Tomas. Who had a grudge against him so big it was worth gunning him down for?'

'If I told you, it would only be guesswork.'

'Guess away.' Marcie tried to tough it out, but underneath she was as scared as Lola and me.

'It could've been one of half a dozen guys,' Lola began. 'Really, Marcie, you've no idea what it's like inside a professional sport: the pressure, what people will do to get to the top.'

'So enlighten me.'

'Winning is everything. Pushing yourself to the limit and then beyond. Realising that you're good, knowing that there's someone better coming up behind you.' Lola told it wearily, her voice muffled by the damp walls. Her face was just visible in the chink of light that crept in under the metal door, so what you concentrated on was her eyes.

'And the pressure pushes you down roads you don't want to go?' I prompted. We knew this already, so I wanted her to get to the bit where she talked about Lendlova.

'Yeah. And you build up grudges against some players.

You try not to, you tell yourself this is only a game.'

Marcie and me; we laughed at this. 'Only a game!' we echoed. So how come we were facing elimination big-time?

'For instance, everyone in the Women's game is afraid of Bernice Matthieu. She's the one you don't want to be drawn against, the one you don't talk with in the locker room.'

'But I heard you planned to be her doubles partner.' This didn't fit with the picture being painted.

'Tomas,' Lola said quietly. 'He made me. He fixed it up with Alain Matthieu. Those two went way back. At one time they were very close.'

'So why pull out?'

'Because . . . because, like I said, I don't like Bernice.'

'She sounded upset when you went missing,' I told her, remembering the interview she gave after she won her second round match.

'Crocodile tears,' Lola assured me. 'Bernice doesn't give a damn about any of the other players on the circuit. So anyway, I stood up to Tomas and told him I wouldn't partner her. Which is when he first went crazy at me. He said I shouldn't rock the boat, that we'd win the doubles tournament, no contest, and that Alain would be upset with me if I let Bernice down.'

'That sounds scary!' Marcie picked up the word 'upset'

and the implications behind it.

'Worse than you could possibly know.' Lola paused. Even down here in the dungeon, she was looking over her shoulder to make sure no one could hear. 'When I say Tomas and Alain went way back, it was to the 1980s and the drugs scandal in Men's tennis. Alain was caught, but Tomas wasn't. Alain refused to implicate him, so Tomas owed him plenty.'

'You mean, when Alain got out of gaol, Tomas had to do everything he told him?' I got this part of the picture at least. 'And when you suddenly pulled out of the doubles, Matthieu leaned on your uncle to persuade you to change your mind?'

Lola nodded. 'Yeah, but once I made my decision, I stuck with it. Tomas tried to get at me through my mom and dad, thinking they could persuade me. But, you know, I felt good. For the first time I'd stood up to them all. I thought, " *This is how it should be; me making my own decisions.*" '

'Good on you!' Marcie murmured.

We heard the truck start up and roll slowly away from the demolition site overhead.

'So you said no to the plastic envelope also.' I took up the thread again before we fell back into a long silence. 'Then what?'

'What I didn't know until last weekend, after the

basketball final, was exactly how much Tomas was under Alain's control. He freaked out when I said no to the performance enhancers, because he said it would lessen Bernice's and my chances of winning the doubles. He said Matthieu would get to hear and then his own situation would suffer. I said, what did I care any more? I was my own person now. I would go to the sport's governing body and tell them about everything: the drugs, how the Matthieus terrified people into doing what they wanted them to do.'

'Oh my God!' Marcie said slowly. 'You think this message somehow got back to the Matthieus?'

'Yes, and I think they had a big argument and blamed Tomas, and that's why he was shot.' Lola laid it on the line, her voice shaking.

(*'Matthew*. Game, set and match.'

Or, *'Matthieu*. Game, set and match.'

Jeez! My mind exploded like a firecracker. *Kate, get here fast. I have to talk to you about a vital error we both made.*)

'It's not your fault!' Marcie whispered, holding Lola's hand as she began to cry.

Whose fault it was didn't really matter now, I realised, as I heard a set of footsteps approaching above. Footsteps crunching across dirt and rubble, stopping at the door. Then a key turned in the lock, and my only thought was to grab Lola and Marcie and pin them back against the wall.

I waited for a flashlight to shine down the steps, thinking that it sounded like only one man who would be expecting us still to be tied and gagged. So maybe we could use the element of surprise. Maybe we could spring out, overpower him and escape.

'C'mon!' I thought, willing him to open that door. *'Shine that beam, baby. Just give us the glimmer of a chance to get the hell out of here!'*

13

Starkweather took me in the car with her and Wade. The siren wailed through Marytown into the city centre, got us across Constitution Square and out along West Grand Street towards Fairview.

'Get me three squad cars out to the industrial estate!' Wade barked into his radio, steering and yelling instructions at the same time, swearing at guys in delivery vans who failed to heed the siren. You wouldn't believe the traffic chaos one blue flashing light and one wailing siren can cause.

Ladies in pastel-coloured convertibles freak out and wobble across your path. Truck drivers get jammed at angles of forty-five degrees across junctions, blocking the lights and stacking up traffic for hundreds of yards.

Wade just swore some more and rode the sidewalks, '*Waah-waah-waah!*'

Over my shoulder I glimpsed Angel's car following in our wake. It contained Dad and the Carters. The Kodaks were behind them in a taxi. Boy, could that cab-driver squeeze through some small spaces.

So, we were out of the city and speeding through miles of bungalows. The streets were wide and deserted, we were jumping lights, making good time.

And all this – Wade stampeding through a residential estate in an afternoon heat-haze, calling three back-up cars to meet him in Fairview – was on a hunch, a slim possibility. I mean, if I was Alain Matthieu and I was holding three kids hostage, I wouldn't sit them in the smart reception block of my sportswear company, on view to the world.

'OK?' Starkweather checked with me. She kept her head as the sergeant narrowly missed a black dog and an old guy on a bicycle crossing the street.

My knuckles were white as they gripped the seat in front. But I nodded. Compared with Carter and the girls, my situation was hunky-dory.

The industrial estate sat in a dip between two steep, wooded hillsides. It wasn't new and smart. In fact, some of the units were so old they were abandoned and falling down, there was grass growing through cracks in the road surface and there were half a dozen big but faded 'For Rent' signs covered in graffiti that must have been there for years while the units quietly crumbled.

But there was a computer software place with hundreds of cars parked outside, and a furniture manufacturer with a big display room, so some of these units were still doing good business.

'Look out for a big sign saying "Pro-Sport",' Starkweather urged as Wade turned off the light and siren, slowed from 70 to 50 and cruised quietly between the units.

'There!' I pointed to six-foot-high neon lettering perched on top of a building next door to a demolition site. The factory was one of the units that seemed to be pulling the estate back from the brink. It was low-rise, clean and graffiti-free, approached by a curving drive edged by trimmed lawn. At the end of the drive there was a smart reception, inviting you in to sit and wait for your appointment in its grey leather chairs surrounding its shiny steel coffee tables.

To be frank, when I stepped out of the cop car with Wade and Starkweather, I couldn't help feeling that coming here had been a major mistake. This was too normal, too workaday; no way would we find what we were looking for here.

Maybe Angel and the others thought so too, because I noticed them hang back then stop at a polite distance from the Pro-Sport entrance. They had obviously decided to park on the sidewalk by the demolition site and wait and see. Likewise, the first squad car that showed up in response to Wade's urgent call.

'Let's go.' The sergeant was the first through the door into reception, bull-neck disappearing into his broad shoulders and barrel-chest. He flashed his ID at the girl at the desk and snapped out a request to speak with Mr Alain Matthieu.

She was halfway through telling him that Mr Matthieu wasn't in the office today when the man himself walked out of the room behind her.

Alan Matthieu; blond, tanned and confident. Too confident to need to smile and shake hands, or to pretend to be surprised by a visit from the cops. No; he approached Wade in a businesslike way, ignoring Starkweather and me.

I, meanwhile, was staring at him. He was so good-looking he must have spent his whole life transfixing people, especially women. More than six feet tall, everything in proportion. If this had been Ancient Greece, he would have modelled for the statue of a god. If he'd chosen a career in films, he would've made the 'A' list of male leads. I mean it; this guy was stunning.

Chunky little Wade was, of course, unimpressed. He took pictures of Carter and Marcie out of his pocket and showed them to Matthieu, politely reminding him in addition that Lola Kodak was still a missing person and suggesting that the Frenchman might be able to help in their inquiries on all three individuals.

Matthieu frowned and led us into his office. 'What can I say?' he shrugged. 'We'd all like this mystery about Lola to be cleared up as quickly as possible. I'll do anything I can to help.'

'Where were you yesterday afternoon, around 4.00pm?' Wade asked, point-blank.

The room was comfortably air-conditioned, even though the heat of the sun beating down on the sprinkled lawns outside was intense. I noticed the fine jets spraying the grass turn to brilliant diamonds in the bright rays. They partly obscured the row of cars parked beyond, but I did pick out a long, low, black, executive-type saloon.

So did Starkweather. She murmured in Wade's ear and left the room, with me close on her heels.

We were out through reception, standing on the drive in the full glare of the sun when the first shot was fired.

It came from the abandoned lot next door, across a wasteland of broken glass, heaps of crumbling bricks, tall purple weeds.

Starkweather recognised what it was and hit the ground, wresting her own gun out of its holster as she dropped. She held it in a double grip, pointed across the wasteground. 'Get down!' she yelled at me.

But the crack of gunfire continued. It stunned and confused me, pushed me over the edge into craziness. (*Joey! For God's sake, Joey!*)

I ran across the smooth lawn, feeling the cold spray of the sprinklers soak through my shirt, then I battled through some spiked bushes on to the demolition site.

I was in time to see two men with guns race through a derelict building. The windows were empty holes, the top storey had begun to crumble, and the steps to the main entrance tilted at a lopsided angle and failed to meet the door.

But that wasn't where the guys with the guns were headed. They split up at the corner of the building, pointing and firing as they ran. Overhead, on the crumbling first storey, I saw a figure climb up an old staircase and sprint away from the gunshots.

Joey! Yes, it was him making space between himself and the bullets! I kept my mouth shut, jumped over a heap of old bricks and tangled razor-wire and kept on heading for the shell of the old factory.

I had the hazy impression of other things going on: of car doors slamming and distant sirens drawing nearer, of footsteps closing in. And more gunfire. I heard bullets ricochet off walls, saw Joey still running along the upper level, heading for the far end of the building.

Then Marcie and Lola burst out of a hole in the ground, near to where I had first caught sight of the gunmen. It was practically under my feet, half-covered by sheets of rusting metal, so that I hadn't seen the worn stone steps leading underground until I was on top of the thing and the girls scrambled out, blinded by the sun, running with their hands to their faces without any sense of direction.

'This way!' I yelled, grabbing Lola's arm.

I led them, stumbling, across the bricks and glass into Starkweather's safekeeping.

Marcie was screaming Joey's name, turning and trying to run back. 'He's still over there!' she cried, pulling and wrenching. But the detective kept tight hold of her until more help arrived.

I was gone again, back across the wasteland. By this time, both gunmen had met up on the staircase to the first storey and were following Joey, confident now that they had him trapped with no means of escape.

Heart thumping, gasping for breath, I stayed at ground level and ran the length of the old factory until I came to the end where I'd last seen Joey. I looked up directly into the sun's glare, shaded my eyes and saw him peering through an empty window frame at a thirty-foot drop on to cracked concrete.

He had only seconds to make his escape. The

gunmen had slowed to a silent prowl, their figures visible whenever they passed across a crumbling window frame, arms outstretched, keeping Joey in their sights.

'Stand clear, I'm gonna jump!' he warned me.

'You'll kill yourself! Joey, don't do it!' The sun glinted behind him, blinding me.

'If I don't, those guys will shoot anyway!' He clambered out on to the stone ledge, teetering on the edge. His arms waved madly as he fought to keep his balance, crouching, ready to make the leap into space.

'. . . Don't anybody move!'

I spun round from Joey to look at Wade.

The detective sergeant wasn't alone. He stood behind me on the concrete yard holding a stubby but deadly gun to the head of Alain Matthieu.

'Tell your gorillas to throw down their weapons,' Wade told him calmly. 'Because if anyone's gonna get caught in stray gunfire around here, it could be you.'

'What the hell do you think you were doing, Joey Carter?' I turned on him as the cops swarmed over Matthieu and his two hitmen, yelling at the top of my voice.

'Staying alive.' He had taken the safe way down to ground level via the staircase, and was brushing brick dust from his arms and T-shirt while arrests were made.

Across the piles of rubble, his mom and dad had set off at a run towards us.

Starkweather had let go of Marcie and Lola and they'd staggered back to the concrete yard.

'He saved us!' Lola cried. 'He jumped the first guy as soon as he flashed his light down the basement steps!'

'I didn't know there were two of them, did I?' Joey muttered. 'I knocked the flashlight out of the first guy's hand and brought him crashing down the steps. But the second one took me by surprise. I made a run for it, hoping that I could draw them both away from the basement.'

'Giving us time to get out of that black hole,' Lola said, shivering and crying. Delayed shock was getting to her and Marcie, and they were still having a hard time adjusting to the bright light.

'You're crazy!' I yelled at Carter. 'You have no right getting mixed up in stuff like this – guns, bullets, guys who shoot without even thinking about it!'

He stopped cleaning his clothes then and looked up at me. 'I noticed you keeping a safe distance . . . *Not!*'

'That's different,' I stammered.

Dad and Angel, Dr and Mrs Kodak had joined with the Carters in the sprint to join us. We'd soon be awash with family scolding and hugging, crying all over us.

'. . . I thought you were gonna get yourself killed!' I could have grabbed the idiot by the neck of that grime-streaked T-shirt.

'Well, I didn't.'

'But you could've . . .' I wanted to throw my arms around him, do the hugging and crying myself.

But Mrs Carter flung herself at her son and smothered him in tears. Dad caught me by the shoulders and held me close. Marcie had her dad to take care of her, and Lola was weeping in her mother's arms.

UPDATE

So Kate and I missed our chance. So, what's new?

Angel, being the go-for-it type, got her exclusive interview with Lola Kodak. Lola took a couple of days to think about things, then announced to the Angel-works crew that she'd decided after all to return to the professional tennis circuit.

There was a lot of stuff about her owing it to her fans to continue, and the fact that the game would be a lot cleaner now that Matthieu's drugs ring had been broken. She put on a public show of supporting her parents while they straightened out their so-called mistakes with the Internal Revenue people. Privately, Lola told Marcie that she forgave her mother but not her father. There was talk of a divorce. Lola said, as far as she was concerned, she was happy never to see Dr Kodak ever again.

I'll think of that whenever I read about her winning Wimbledon or the Australian Open. Which I know she will.

She promised Marcie to keep in touch this time. Which I also know she will.

Bernice Matthieu pulled out of the championship at Flushing Meadow. She admitted taking drugs to enhance her performance and was dropped from the Women's rankings within twenty-four hours of her husband's arrest.

Don't waste any tears. If you ask me, she deserves as long a gaol sentence as Alain Matthieu's gonna get when his case comes to court. In this state we don't have the death sentence, even for Murder One.

Kate says she's relieved about this, not wanting the responsibility of sending Matthieu to the chair. I agree maybe 99.9% because I'm a civilised type. But 0.1% remembers that dark hole in the ground and bullets ripping past my head.

We went back to school the next day; Friday.

Zig gave me a ticket for a big baseball game. Thanks, Zig.

Slay saw Kate coming down the corridor and bulldozed her against the girls' lockers.

'What happened to you, Kate Brennan?' she yelled, eyeball to eyeball. 'What cropped up that was so life-threateningly urgent to make you miss yesterday's tennis match against East Village High?'

FOUR FOR A BOY

Jenny Oldfield

Kate Brennan, Joey Carter.
Flirting with danger ... and each other

A homeless boy, a body dumped by the railway tracks. For the police, just another violent street death. But Carter knew the murdered boy and won't let it rest. He and Kate enter a world where the illegal roll of the dice brings danger. And powerful politicians stack the odds against them.

FIVE FOR SILVER

Jenny Oldfield

Kate Brennan. Joey Carter.
Flirting with danger . . . and each other.

A despised school principal meets a
sudden, violent end. So what? Carter and
Kate don't lose much sleep over the brutal
murder – until their friend and recently
excluded pupil, Kurt Silvermann, becomes
a prime suspect. And the widow's offer of
a $5,000 reward thrusts them into a
dangerous race to clear his name . . .